FLEE

By

Miranda Kavi

Chapter 1

I can fly. It's not as cool as it sounds. Actually, it really sucks.

"Are you sure you can handle this?" my mom asked.

"I'm a grown up now. Right?"

"Right." She didn't look convinced. She leaned forward to give me a peck on the cheek. "I'm so proud of you. Who would have ever thought my little girl would go to law school?"

"All right, all right." I tossed my purse into the front seat of my battered old car. "I should go."

Her green eyes followed me as I got in. I rolled down the window. She hovered nearby, arms crossed over her chest. She still wore her light blue scrubs from the night shift. Her hair, a pretty light blond unlike my chestnut brown, was pulled into a ponytail.

"Okay. Off I go." I turned the key in the ignition.

She leaned in my open window, her face serious again. "Don't let your guard down. I'm still not sure about this."

"Mom, I'll be okay. I can't stay in Wichita my whole life. We talked about this." I kept the gear in neutral, but tapped the gas to rev the engine. "I need to go."

She studied the back seat of my car, filled with boxes and bags. "Are you sure you can see out the back window? Is your cell phone charged? If you can't make the drive all in one day, just pull over."

"Mom, please. I do need to go. Today would be best."

"Fine, kiddo. Love you." Her smile was weak, but it was there. She pressed several twenties into my hand. "Bye!"

I saluted her and then drove away.

৯৽৽৻

Exactly forty-eight hours later, I stood in a small crowd of strangers. Many fingered the collars of starched dress shirts and fidgeted with ties in the humidity and Texas heat. It was the first day of law school. Orientation leaders had divided us into small groups to tour the campus, get our schedules, and pick up books.

"I feel like I'm back in high school, but we're the nerdy, overdressed freshman," I whispered to Bree, a friendly girl who I'd been chatting with all day. She was built similar to me – short and petite. Her hair was platinum blond and short and her eyes were a bright blue.

She leaned closer to me to answer. "Agreed. Have you noticed all the 2L's and 3L's here are in shorts and flip flops? They probably told us to dress up so we would look like complete morons and they could have a cheap laugh."

"2L?"

"Yeah. We're 1L's, first year law students. A 2L is a second year law student, a 3L is a third year law student."

"How did you even know that? It's the first day and I'm already out of the loop." I used the campus map to fan my face.

She snickered. "You're not out of the loop. I read it on some message board."

We followed our guide out of the bookstore. He paused to point out some of the other buildings on the campus. The white stone chapel dominated this end of the campus. It had a statue of the Virgin Mary in front of it, surrounded by what was probably a very pretty courtyard. Right now, vans, cameras, and trailers were piled inside the perimeter. Large silver screens leaned against the side of the building.

"Are they filming something there?" I asked Bree.

"Huh. Looks like it." She raised her voice. "Um, excuse me, tour guide person?"

He pivoted to face her. "For the fourth time, my name is Joseph. See?" He pointed to his nametag.

"Okay, Joseph. I have a question. Are they filming something here?"

"Yes. It's the movie adaptation of *Blue Leaf*. They're filming at the University and some of the old missions around town."

"Are there any famous people here?" a very sweaty guy in a suit asked.

Joseph shrugged. "Supposedly, but I haven't seen any."

"Like who?" I asked.

"Try Mira Tavana, Savannah Gessner, Troy Archili and Gavyn Dhaval on for size." I turned to the speaker. She was tall, tan, and carrying a handbag worth at least four times as much as my car. "You haven't heard? Everyone is talking about it."

"No. Just got here today. Right?" Bree turned her back on the girl. I smiled at her, but followed Bree as she walked away.

We walked in the heat to the part of campus housing the law school structures.

"Have you noticed anything odd about this place?" Bree asked as we climbed the stairs of the main law school building.

"Well, besides the awesome taco stands, a bunch of spoiled twenty-two-year-olds who drive luxury cars, and the unbearable heat?"

"Something far more sinister. There are no hot guys. None. Absolutely none."

I laughed so loud people stared at us. "Maybe it will get better when school starts for real and all the other students are here." I pulled the rubber band off my wrist and used it to tie my long hair up off my neck.

"I freakin' hope so."

We walked into the large and wonderfully air conditioned building that held the majority of the classrooms for the law school. Long folding tables lined the wall of the lobby, manned with 2L's and 3L's handing out schedules. I got into the "A-L" line so I could get my schedule.

Bree found me leaned against the cool stone wall reviewing my classes.

"Okay. So there are eight sections. Which one are you?" She stood on her tiptoes to peek at my schedule. She's one of the few people in the world shorter than me.

"Er...blue, I think."

"Sweet! Me too. Our schedules will be identical."

"Cool. I guess I'll see you tomorrow." I shouldered my way too heavy backpack. She was nice, but I wasn't the type to have close friends. As my mom always said, it's easy to keep a secret when you don't have anyone to share it with.

I walked out the glass double doors, relieved to be alone again. The hot weather hurt my lungs. It was like walking in an oven. The oven turned into an incinerator once I got in my car.

I jacked the AC as high up as it could go. It moved the air around in the car, but it wasn't cool yet. I used the back of my hand to wipe a layer of sweat off my forehead. "Yucky."

My car offered a squeal of protest as I pulled out of the parking lot. The side streets surrounding the campus were crowded with early evening traffic.

I rolled to a stop at the first stoplight. I heard the sickening crunch before I felt the impact.

"Crap." I glanced in my rearview mirror at the dark blue car now attached to the back of mine. I did a quick self-check. Nothing was hurt or bleeding. I tried to get out of my car, but my door was stuck closed. I pounded on it with my shoulder until it popped open.

I tumbled out, and ran smack into a solid, warm body. "Oof."

"Are you all right? Should I call an emergency vehicle?" His voice was soft, but with a heavy British accent. He wrapped a strong hand around my arm and pulled me off the ground.

"Emergency vehicle?" I echoed. I dragged my eyes up to his face. He was wearing sunglasses. Wild black hair escaped in tendrils from the dark gray knit cap pulled down over his ears. He was lean, muscular, and dreamy. His t-shirt strained around his broad shoulders.

He smiled, and it was perfect. "Or, ambulance, whatever you call it here. Are you okay?"

"Yeah, I am. Do you require emergency vehicular assistance?" As I tried to flirt, I remembered I was covered in sweat and wearing an unflattering pair of slacks and suit jacket. My nametag with the law school's logo clung to my lapel.

His smile got wider, but he dropped his hand away from my arm. "Not today. I'm fine, Miss,"—he moved closer to read my name tag— "Lockette?"

I met his eyes again. My train of thought evaporated. "Um, yes. What happened?" I shielded my eyes from the fading sun to examine the wreckage.

"My driver said the brakes failed and we slammed right into you. I will see to it personally you are compensated accordingly. I am very sorry."

"You have a driver?" I said.

A burly man wearing a cap approached us. "Miss, I'm the driver of that vehicle." He pointed at the dark blue car. "Are you okay? Should we exchange insurance info? I've already called the police."

"Sure." I retrieved the insurance info out of the glove box. A nice traffic jam was forming behind us, one car at a time squeezing past the wreckage. To my dismay, several of the cars contained fellow law students who had plenty of time to take in my wrecked piece-of-crap car and my sweaty, distraught appearance.

I leaned against the door and closed my eyes. My legs and arms were shaking. I needed to concentrate to keep it from happening. I counted back from twenty, picturing each number as it passed through my concentration. The calm came, slowly at first, but then I felt normal. My feet remained firmly planted on earth's surface.

"Miss? The insurance?" The driver was standing in front of me. "Are you okay?"

I straightened my posture. "I am. Thank you. Here you go." I gave him a copy of my insurance card. He plopped it down on the trunk of my car and began copying over the information to a notebook.

My emergency lights were flashing and it was starting to get dark. I sat on the curb and kicked off my heels while we waited for the police. I closed my eyes and tried to find my happy place, which right now was anywhere but here.

It occurred to me it might look weird for me to sit shoeless on a street curb with my eyes closed, so I opened them. The handsome British guy had one sneakered foot on the curb, just a few feet away from me. He had removed his hat and sunglasses, revealing light brown eyes and matching caramel colored skin. He was ridiculously handsome. And rich, judging by the luxury car now entangled with my economy ride and the fact he had a driver.

He looked vaguely familiar. I racked my brain, trying to place him. *Oh, my God.* Shock rippled through me when I realized who he was: Gavyn Dhaval. The lead actor of *Blue Leaf* Gavyn Dhaval.

He was watching me. His eyes met mine and he smiled. I smiled back, a little embarrassed I was caught staring.

My smile must have been an invitation, because he closed the space between us. "Why don't we go inside, Ms. Lockette? I'm sure he'll come get us when the police officers get here." He gestured at the small Mexican restaurant halfway down the block.

"It's Aurora, and yes, let's go inside. I'm hot." I flushed at the double meaning of the words, but managed to retrieve my handbag from the ground, put on my shoes in relative short order and follow him into the restaurant. The air conditioning was nothing short of heaven.

The food was delivered five minutes after we ordered. I stared at my plate in silence. My stomach was sour and food didn't seem like a good idea anymore. I took the opportunity to remove my suit jacket, straighten my blouse, and use some napkins to dab my sweat soaked face.

"So, Aurora. What do you do?"

"I'm a law student."

"Law student? Hmmm." His beautiful smile came back full force. "Aren't you going to ask me what I'm doing here?"

I took a bite of my food while I gathered my thoughts. "I was getting there. What's your name?"

"Gavyn."

"And what do you do, Mr. Gavyn?"

He leaned back in his chair and chuckled softly. "You're funny. Where are you from?"

My thoughts scattered. He was way too good looking. "I'm not really from anywhere, but right now I live here," I answered after a too-long pause for such a simple question.

"What do you mean you're not really from anywhere?"

"Well, I move around a lot. I don't have a place I would call home, well, except maybe for Kansas. I lived there for ten years. What about you? Where are you from?"

"London. Born and raised, but my father is from India." He scooted his chair closer. "Pardon my staring, but you have the most unusual eyes. Gray, like a dark storm cloud. Very beautiful."

I felt the heat rush to my face. "Storm cloud, huh? Thanks." I pushed my food around my plate, desperate to fill the silence. "So, your dad is from India?"

"Yep. My mom's British. They met in college."

My palms, one of my few hold out non-sweating parts, were sweating now too.

"So, what exactly does being a law student entail? I'm afraid I am completely unfamiliar with the American legal education system," he said.

"Just started. Ask me in a week."

He threw back his head and laughed. After a moment, he took another bite of his meal. I took the opportunity to take a bite of my forgotten food.

"You,"—he paused before continuing—"are very interesting."

"In a boring law student sort of way, I suppose you're right." I forced myself to take another bite of my meal, thinking of ways to continue to be interesting to him. "Does that mean I don't get to hear about what you're doing?"

The driver appeared in the doorway and motioned for us to come. "Police are here. They want to talk to you."

I stood up too fast, knocking over my near empty water glass in the process. I snatched it up, which resulted in my fork flying off the table. "Excuse me. Nice to meet you, Gavyn, and thanks for the burrito."

He picked up my fork and placed it near my plate. "Pleasure was mine."

The tiredness and stress of the day was buzzing in my body. I had to be careful, or else it would happen. I focused on calming down, keeping my cool, and my feet planted on the ground.

My thoughts bounced around aimlessly while I waited for the police officer to finish his report. I'd just met a movie star, which was great. Unfortunately, I met him in a too-large discount suit, covered in sweat, and God only knows how bad my hair was at this point. Did I flirt? More importantly, did he flirt?

Hours later, I finally arrived at my apartment in a compact red rental car I couldn't really afford. I flopped on the bed and examined the textured ceiling. I couldn't believe I had a conversation with Gavyn Dhaval. The most amazing part was he seemed like a normal guy. Definitely not the narcissistic snob I would have expected.

Too bad I would never see him again, except maybe on a movie screen.

I turned off the light, effectively ending my daydreaming.

Chapter 2

My laptop sputtered to life in front of me, joining row after row of glowing computer screens. A few holdout students had notebooks and pencils instead. We all had red bound, obnoxiously thick textbooks parked on our desks.

Our civil procedure professor was standing in the front of the room, trying to clip a small microphone to his button-down shirt.

I opened my internet browser and searched for "Gavyn Dhaval." His picture spread across my screen. There were many fan sites and links to movies he had done, but not a lot of tabloid stories.

"Hey!" Bree sat down next to me and booted up her laptop. I clicked all my windows shut to get Gavyn's face off my screen, and hopefully, my mind.

She scooted her computer close to mine and typed. *Hey. This will be a lot easier than passing notes.*

Yep, except everyone behind us can read them, I wrote back on my screen.

She messed with her settings then started typing again, this time in a much smaller font. *Can you hear me now?* ☺

Yep. Isn't it weird to have all the same classes with the same exact people?

Yeah, especially since there are only three cute guys in our section, of which two are checking you out right now.

She gestured her head to the right. Sure enough, two guys sitting next to each other on the other side of the classroom were watching us openly and smiling. One with broad shoulders and sandy brown hair, one smaller guy who had spiky blond hair.

I nudged Bree and wrote, *Checking you out, blondie.*

She wrote back, *Checking us out . . .*

A loud tap on his lapel where the microphone was, and the professor had our attention. "All right, section blue. Let's get started. I'm Professor Tolane, and this is Federal Rules of Civil Procedure."

I poised my hands above my keyboard, ready to capture every word, when it happened. The buzzing sensation started in my head, and then quickly flowed down my body into my hands and feet. I felt my bottom rise out of the chair a fraction of an inch.

Concentrate, Aurora. I wrapped my hands around the bottom of my seat to keep myself firmly attached. *Not here, not in front of everyone, not so soon.* I pictured the numbers in my head, 20, 19, 18, counting backward. Once I had the calm, the control followed easily. 17, 16, 15...

An elbow dug into my side. I opened my eyes.

"Excuse me, Ms. Lockette?" The professor was standing in front of me. "Because according to the seating chart, this is you."

I cleared my throat. "Yes. I'm me. I mean, I'm here."

"And, what is your answer, Miss. Lockette?"

"Answer?"

"Stand up please."

I did.

"While you were resting, we were discussing jurisdiction." The other students shifted awkwardly in their seats, the girl from yesterday's tour group tittered, and my face burned. "What was the holding from Louisville & Nashville Railroad v. Mottley?"

"Um..." I flipped through the case book. The pages I had read last night for all my different classes were jumbling together. "A court has federal jurisdiction only if the plaintiff's cause of action arises under the constitution or federal statutes."

He smiled, but it wasn't a friendly smile. "As opposed to..."

"Federal jurisdiction based on the defendant's counterclaim under the federal statutes or constitution."

"Right. Stay standing please. I'll come back to you. No cat naps in my class."

He turned his attention away and continued his lecture, while I stood like a Grade-A moron. Wonderful. I glanced down at Bree's screen. She had written "Welcome to Law School."

≈≈

Back in the sunlight, I sipped on a bottle of water while I flipped through the cases for my next class. I was seated at one of the many tables scattered around the campus. Bree sat next to me, along with a tall, quiet guy she had somehow befriended within the past few hours.

Masses of law students streamed in and out of the buildings. They gathered in clusters around the tables to chug down coffee, smoke, and socialize.

I had finished my reading by now, but I pretended I was still working. Bree and the quiet guy were engaged in conversation. I let my eyes flow over the page as I wrestled with my internal worry over the classroom incident.

I shut my book. "I'm going to head to the gym. See you later."

Bree flipped open her cell phone and looked at the screen. "You have two hours until your next class. Come eat with us instead."

"Thanks for the invite, but I'll pass."

The gym was on the other side of the campus. Basketball and racquetball courts filled the first level while the second level offered cardio machines and weights.

It only took me a second to change out of my jeans and t-shirt into sneakers, shorts, and a rattier t-shirt. I pulled my hair into a ponytail as I made my way to the weight room.

It was empty, which was awesome. I selected twenty-pound dumbbells and got to work. Calm and focus washed through my body and cleared my mind. Just what I needed.

I wandered over to the bench press. I selected a twenty-pound disc from the stack near the bench, and added one to each side. I added more weight in smaller increments, not sure of how much I could handle without assistance.

"Need a spot?" a friendly voice asked. He looked familiar, but he couldn't be older than eighteen or nineteen. He was Hispanic, muscular, and very cute in the high school jock sort of way and had a big, open smile on his face.

"Thanks."

He stood over me while I performed my limited repetitions.

"Nice job," he said as I slowly returned to an upright position. "I'm Troy by the way. What's your name?"

"Aurora. Nice to meet you."

"Like the northern lights? Very cool. Are you working on the movie, or are you a student 'round here?"

Something clicked in my brain. Troy Archili. Another lead in the movie. Currently sharing the cover of a prominent magazine with one of his former co-stars. I'm not sure when I'd been transported to a much cooler alternate dimension where I met movie stars on a daily basis.

I cleared my throat and found my voice. "Student. Not a movie star. Sorry to disappoint."

His smile grew even broader. "What's your major, non-movie star?"

"I'm a law student."

"Oh, really? You don't look it. You're too short."

I laughed. "Thanks, I think."

His smile faded a little. "I hope I get to go to college someday. I'm pretty much booked for the next few years, though."

"That's a good thing, right? You can go later, when you're done being famous."

"Ha ha, lawyer. I like you. Now finish those reps." He pointed his finger at the bench.

I saluted him and returned to the bench to finish my reps.

"Holler at me if you need another spot," he said. He tossed me a wave as he returned to the dumbbell rack. He was safe. Not flirty, just friendly.

As I finished my workout and prepared to leave, he stepped in front of me. "Hey."

"Hi," I said.

"So, what are you working on tomorrow?"

"Probably quads and hamstrings."

"Me too. Same place same time?"

"Sure," I said.

"Awesome."

I was smiling as I walked back to the law school area of campus, fresh from my quick shower. Stress was gone. Control was back. Maybe even a new friend?

I walked behind the main campus library and rounded the corner to return to the law school.

"Oomph." I ran into a solid body.

"Are you going to make a habit of this?" he said in his low voice. Even behind the large sunglasses and a baseball cap, I recognized him. He waved a hand, and two large men at his side backed off several feet.

"I'm so sorry." I took a step back so I wasn't standing in his space. I ran my fingers through my hair to straighten it, but I hadn't re-applied makeup after my workout so I still looked less than stellar. "But really, you literally ran into the back of my car, so..."

"Are you going to sue me?" A smile tugged at one corner of his mouth.

"We'll see."

"Where were you headed?" He peered around me so he could see my backpack. "That looks a little heavy."

I slung it off and put it on the ground. "It is heavy, but I've gotta take three books to one class. It's ridiculous."

"When is your class?"

"About ten minutes from now," I said.

"Well, we better get going." He picked up my backpack and walked off.

"What are you doing?" I ran a few steps to catch up to him.

"I'm carrying your books to class for you. I'm trying to repay you for the trouble I caused with the car accident." He winked at me and slipped his other arm through the backpack so it was balanced on both shoulders. "Wow! How do you manage this?"

"I work out." I tried to ignore the heavy footsteps behind us. I leaned close to him. "Are those your bodyguards?" I stage whispered.

He glanced back. "Yep."

"How very odd," I said.

His smile darkened. "Odd, indeed. The studio requires them. I think their insurance makes them do it. I'm quite embarrassed. Please excuse them."

He stopped in the tree grove behind the law school campus. "Here you go." He took off the backpack.

"Are you not allowed on the law campus?" I asked.

He leaned forward so his face was close to mine. "I'm very sorry. I avoid crowds of people."

"Me too," I said, and it was honest.

He cocked his head to the side. "And why is that?"

"I need to get to class. Thanks for the backpack assistance."

I put on my backpack and walked away. The buzzing sensation was tingling my hands and feet, but this time, I had control.

Chapter 3

It was still dark outside, which is perfectly normal at 5:00 a.m., but observing this early hour was not normal for me. Over the past few weeks, Troy had taken great yet smug joy in becoming my own ad-hoc personal trainer, which involved running before breakfast.

My apartment was on the edge of town, where the flat city landscape bleeds into the beginning of the hill country. There were lots of trees and not a lot of people. I had picked it because it seemed like a peaceful area, but in the pre-dawn dark, it was too quiet.

I walked a few steps before I broke out into a run. Power surged through my legs and arms, quieting the now nearly constant buzzing in my hands and feet. The control came with the exercise, came with the calm.

I'd gone a mile when something nudged at my consciousness. I stopped my run.

Someone was watching me. The buzzing had started, and I was on the verge of losing control. I stared into the shadow-filled trees. Somebody was out there, blending from one tree's shadow to the next to the next in a jerky, unnatural motion.

"Is someone there?"

There was no response.

My feel lifted off the ground a fraction of an inch. Damn it. The figure came closer, not yet detached from the tree line.

Run, stupid. And I did. I sprinted as fast as I could. I didn't hear anyone behind me, but I couldn't hear much over my pounding feet and gasping lungs. As I neared the apartment complex, the fear receded. The lights from the complex wrapped around me, and I was safe again.

I shut the door to my apartment behind me and engaged the deadbolt. I took an old wooden chair and leaned it under the doorknob.

I stood on my tippy-toes behind the chair so I could see out the peephole. Nothing.

I stayed there until my neck hurt from the awkward angle. I turned on all the lights in the apartment and left pepper spray and a cell phone on the sink while I showered. I tried to pretend I hadn't freaked out.

By the time I squeezed my repaired car in-between two nicer ones in the parking lot at school, I was convinced I had imagined the whole thing. I opened my door just enough to get out of my car and squeeze between it and the super expensive car next to it. My bulky backpack made this exercise a challenge.

The owner of the expensive car stood near the bumper of her car with her arms crossed over her unnaturally large chest while she watched me carefully avoid banging her car. I was all nerves, but I smiled while I squeezed past her.

Bree fell into step beside me. "Hey there."

"Hey," I said.

"You want to grab lunch today? We're going to try the deep fried taco place. Apparently, it's a legend around these parts."

"Thanks for the invite, but I'm going to pass."

She grabbed my arm and forced me to stop. "How come you never come with us?"

I retracted my arm. "I'm sorry. Nothing personal. I'm just not good with people."

She pivoted so she was facing me. Since we were both short, I had nowhere else to look but at her face. "That's a crock of shit and you know it. Secretly a man? Terminally ill? You can tell me."

I laughed and took a step back. "None of the above. I have a workout at two today, and fried tacos, whatever those are, are not in my meal plan."

She narrowed her eyes at me for a second. "Fine, but you better avail yourself to us on some weekend."

"Done," I said.

She seemed satisfied because she whirled around and started walking again. "Do you have a trainer or something? I swear you're always at the gym. I haven't been over there yet."

"Kind sorta. I have a workout buddy who helps me out."

"Law student? I haven't seen you really hanging out with anyone."

"No, not a law student."

"An undergrad? Oh, cougar, here me roar!" She made a snarling noise.

I laughed with her. "It's nothing. He's just a friend."

"You said 'he'...I knew it. Gym buddy is a he."

"Like I said, not like that."

"Right." We both walked into Torts class, effectively ending our conversation.

❧⚘

After classes, I found myself leaned up against the back wall of the administrative building. It was cool and shady and there were no people.

I found a small bench nestled against the building, facing the tree grove which backed up against the campus. I pulled a textbook and highlighter out of my backpack, but they sat in my lap, unused.

I was too busy daydreaming. I thought of the things I would never have, of the normalcy so many people seemed to enjoy. I thought of Gavyn, and hated myself for it.

I flipped open the massive textbook. Reading cases for law school wasn't a simple matter of reading. I needed to be able to point out the facts, the holding, and the dissent. This is where my highlighter and pen came in handy. My book was starting to look like an art project with all my notes and multi-colored highlights.

The world went a shade darker. I looked up. A puffy dark cloud had passed over the bright Texas sun. I scanned the grove of trees, now cast in shadows.

Something moved. Something big.

I jumped out of my seat, sending my book and highlighter flying to the ground with a loud thwack. The creepy-crawly sensation swept through my body.

The sidewalks were empty, but something moved through the shadows of the forest, blending from one tree to the next. It flickered, like bad reception on an old T.V.

I kept my eyes on the dark shape as I crouched to retrieve my book. I put my backpack on the floor, and then used my arm to sweep the objects back into my bag. I re-shouldered it, then turned my back on the shape and ran around the corner.

I was back in the law school courtyard, and there were tons of people. I walked slowly through the crowd, throwing glances back at the tree grove. Whatever it was, I could feel it.

The sun came back out, and everyone else was smiling, laughing. I sat on the front steps of the classroom building until I felt calm again. I had missed my workout with Troy, but at least I could think straight. I switched out my books for my gym bag in my trunk. I took the long way to the gym, staying away from the trees.

I fished out my cell phone while I walked.

She answered on the first ring. "Hey, honey. How are you?"

"Hey, Mom."

"You sound stressed. Are you all right?"

I took a deep breath. "Yes, I'm okay, but something is off."

"What is it?"

"I've been having a hard time here. I feel it almost all the time. I constantly have to think about it so I don't, you know..." I glanced around to make sure I was alone. "So I don't fly."

"How long has this been going on?" she asked.

"Since I got here. Since I left. I don't know."

"Why didn't you tell me?"

22

"I didn't want to worry you." I was close to the gym now. "And there's more."

"What?"

"I think I'm being followed."

"What? What do you mean you're being followed? Who is following you?"

"Aurora! Hey, over here!" It was Troy and his booming, cheery, penetrating voice. I glanced up, instantly taking in the taller, slimmer figure next to him.

"Mom, I have to hang up. I'm sorry."

"What? Wait a second, you need to start from the beginning and tell me every—"

"People here. Can't talk." I snapped the phone shut.

"Hey there, Texas rose." Troy bent down so he could give me a quick hug.

"Hi, Aurora," Gavyn said. He had his hands shoved deep in his pockets, and he looked good. Really good.

"Hi." I had a real smile on my face now.

"Wait, you two know each other? Is this the girl you were telling me..." Troy let his voice trail off when he saw the look on Gavyn's face.

I jumped in to end the uncomfortable silence. "What a small world. Troy, I met Gavyn in a fender bender, and Gavyn, I know Troy through the gym."

Troy was beaming. "Yeah, I know. I heard all about it. I just didn't know it was you."

"What?" I asked.

Gavyn spoke again in his quiet voice. "Mate, come on now."

Troy didn't stop. "Chill out, man. This is my gym buddy. Remember me telling you about her? How crazy is that?"

"Very crazy," Gavyn said.

"Speaking of, where were you today?" Troy said.

"Oh, sorry. I got a little busy with school stuff." I tucked my hair over my shoulder.

"I'm glad I ran into you. I'm having a party this Friday and I want you to come."

"Where will it be?" I asked.

"I'm renting out a huge room at the Glitz on the Riverwalk. It's going to be awesome."

I smiled. "Okay, yeah, I'll be there." I snuck another glance at Gavyn. He was watching me.

"Well, you are single, right? I'll try and invite some of my good looking friends," Troy said.

"I'm single."

"Sweet! Check you later, then. You better be in the gym tomorrow."

"Sure. Bye." I waved at both before walking away.

I made it to the gym, but I was a shaky mess, flushed with something more than the heat. Hot movie stars made me nervous.

I changed into shorts and sneakers and went into the cardio room. I selected the stationary bike. It gave my body something to do, but didn't require a lot of concentration to operate. I had a lot to think about.

Friday rolled around before I barely had time to register the week had passed. Bree and I were sitting in the courtyard. We had one more class to go before the weekend.

"Blast it! It is so freakin' hot!" I twisted my hair into a messy bun and stuck a couple of pencils in it to hold it up.

"Yeah, I know. There isn't a deodorant in the world strong enough to make me feel okay about this weather," she replied. "Does it get this hot in Kansas?"

"Not really. And if it does, it is not this humid," I said.

"Yeah, it's the humidity, right? Dallas gets hot and humid too, but not like this." She took another swig of her water bottle. "So what you doing this weekend?"

"I have a little shin-dig tonight, followed by two days of nothing."

"Whose party?"

"The guy at the gym."

"With the youngins'? Are they going to do body shots and play beer pong?"

"Probably." I so badly wanted to confide in her, to trust her, to tell someone. "There's a guy going who's his friend. I'm interested in him."

"Now this," she said, "is good news. A pretty girl like you gets quite a few looks from the boys, but you seemed to ignore it. Tell me more about this boy." She put her elbows on the table, leaned forward, and rested her chin on her folded hands.

I leaned back in my seat. "It's too early to say much, but his name is Gavyn. He's gorgeous, and I turn into a nervous wreck around him."

"Nervous is good. It means there's chemistry."

"I suppose," I said.

"I suppose? That sounds less then enthusiastic. Didn't you date in college? High school?"

"A little," I said. "I'm not a big dater."

She tilted her chin to the side and watched me. Finally, she spoke. "Where is this going to be? What type of people?"

"It's going to be at a hotel on the Riverwalk. I think it's kind of a rich crowd."

She smiled. "Relax. It's San Antonio. The Riverwalk is super laid-back. You know, flip-flops and shorts sort of thing. Just wear a cute sundress or something. Keep it simple."

"Cool. Thanks."

"Oh, and take a cab down there. Parking is a bitch and it's hard to stay sober. Those margaritas are bigger than your face."

The rest of the day passed in a blur as my excitement built about the party. After rushing home to shower, I flung my closet open, hoping the right thing to wear would magically stand out. While I pondered my outfit, I dried and brushed my hair and dusted a light powder on my skin. I didn't bother with any other makeup beside mascara and lip gloss. I settled on hemp sandals and a simple black sundress that set off my toned arms and shoulders nicely.

The cab dropped me off in front of the Glitz. After some wrong turns through the ultra modern lobby, I found myself outside the suite Troy had indicated in his text message.

I knocked on the door. It flew open beneath my hands.

"Welcome! Beer is in the fridge, hotdogs are on the back patio. Come on in!" Troy said.

"Thanks for the invite."

The huge suite looked more like a large apartment. A sectional occupied most of the right side of the room. The wall facing the Riverwalk was made almost entirely of large windows. Out the windows, a huge deck overlooked the Riverwalk below. Brightly colored umbrellas dotted the patio restaurants, while tourists walked down the winding sidewalks by the river.

Troy walked me into the kitchen and showed me where all the drinks were set up. I grabbed a beer and returned with him to the living room. He introduced me to Savannah Gessner, one of the other leads in the movie. She was beautiful and petite, with thick brunette hair cut into an edgy angled bob. She smiled shyly and shook my hand, asking where I got my sandals from. I fell into an easy conversation with her. After I drained my beer, I returned to the kitchen in search of another.

I found a trashcan against the far wall and threw away my empty beer bottle. I turned around and bumped into Gavyn…again.

He had a beer in each hand, with one extended toward me. "You know, this is literally the third time you've bumped into me. Maybe I shouldn't give you this beer."

I took the offered drink and raised it in a mock toast. "Thanks. I'm done walking into you, I promise. At least for today."

We stood in awkward silence. Troy appeared and thumped Gavyn on the back playfully. "Nice of you to show up, Gavyn. Wonder what brought you out? Speaking of which, Aurora, you look hot. You know how to fill out a dress, girl." He walked off, winking at us as he left.

"Wow. That kid's a trip," I said.

"Yes, he is. He was right though." He paused. "I was hoping you would be here, and you do look positively delectable." He put his hand on the wall next to my head and leaned against the wall, angling his body

27

toward me. This small movement almost caused me to have a coronary. "You called him a kid. How old are you?" His face was only inches away from mine.

"A lady never tells. How old are you?" I hoped my smile was flirtatious, and double hoped I didn't have beer breath.

"I'm twenty-two," he responded. "You're in law school, so you have already completed a four year degree, right? You must be twenty-three or twenty four."

"Yes, twenty-three. I thought you weren't familiar with the American legal education system?"

He shrugged. "How do you like San Antonio so far?"

"Well, it seems pretty cool, but I haven't seen much of it."

My stomach betrayed me by growling.

He took his hand off the wall and leaned back. "Let's get you something to eat."

He followed me out onto the patio. We loaded up our plates with the catered Mexican fusion food, grabbed some bottled water, and sat at one of the tables, joining Troy and some of his friends.

Savannah gave me a warm smile as soon as I sat down. "So, how long is law school?"

"First you have to get a four year degree in any major, and then you go to law school, which is three years. Then you take the bar, and viola! You're a lawyer." I raised my hands and made a grand gesture.

"Is that all?" She giggled. "Seriously, wow. It sounds like a lot of school. I don't know if I could do it."

The conversation flowed and ebbed, much like the waves of tourists walking past the balcony. I focused my gaze over the porch to the

Riverwalk. The sun dipped down the horizon, tinting the water a bright orange and red.

"Let's go check it out." Gavyn stood and offered his arm to me.

"Sure." I practically rocketed out of my chair. I thumped my knee on the table in my haste.

"You all right?" he asked, peering down at my bright red right knee.

"No worries. I never bruise no matter what I do. It's the weirdest thing." As I took his offered arm, everyone was openly staring.

"We'll be back," Gavyn said. "Aurora hasn't had a chance to see the Riverwalk yet."

"Right," Troy said, drawing out the word. "You two kids have fun! Don't fall in."

Gavyn led me to edge of the patio where a narrow wooden staircase twisted down to the Riverwalk.

The walkway was built a couple of stories below the surface of downtown. Muted sounds of traffic floated down the stone walls.

I snuck glances at his profile while we walked and talked. The fading fiery sunset cast his skin as smooth, silky coffee.

He turned to the direction of the hotel. He grabbed my arm and gently spun me so I was facing the same direction he was. I was surprised at how far we'd walked while we were lost in our conversation.

"We should turn around. We don't want to get lost."

Actually, I did want to get lost with him, but I stopped myself from saying it. The fact he was touching me distracted me to a point where I was having difficulty with the English language.

He brushed his fingertips lightly down the length of my arm then entwined his fingers with mine. "Is this okay?"

"Yes."

We walked in silence, hand in hand. I battled through all the different emotions rolling around in my head: desire, fear, and a little spark of hope.

We came to a quiet part of the Riverwalk lined with expensive private residences, green ivy, and old stone walls. He released my hand and moved into me. Very, very close. He tucked a stray hair behind my ear, his feathery touch against my skin sending chills down my spine. "I'm not good at this kind of stuff." He was close enough I could feel his breath move across my skin.

"What stuff?"

"You." He raised his eyes to meet mine. "I can't tell if you're into me the same way I'm into you." He moved his hand across my cheek. "I feel for you in a way I haven't before."

"Oh!" I whispered.

His shoulders sunk.

"Let me try again. I'm not good at this stuff either, you see. I really, really like you, and I, um, I wasn't sure if you liked me, and you're famous, and I'm definitely not, and I thought maybe you just went around picking up girls, but I'm not saying you necessarily do that or anything. I thought maybe you were just…"

He cradled my face with his hands. I'm pretty sure my heart stopped beating right then and there. "You weren't sure if I liked you? Really?"

"Yes."

He kissed me. It was the kind of kiss a girl waits a lifetime for. His lips were soft and warm. His hands were gentle, holding my face to his. He moved his hands to wrap them around me, pulling me closer to him and intensifying our kiss. I wrapped my arms around his neck.

After a blissful moment, he pulled away. "Do you have any doubts now?"

"Nope."

He touched his fingers to my lips. "You have such full, beautiful lips; very nice to kiss." He slung one arm over my shoulder and we walked toward the hotel. As we got closer, I could see Troy standing on the balcony, watching the people stream by. I was expecting Gavyn to cease the public display of affection in front of his fellow cast and crew, but he didn't.

When he saw Gavyn's arm around my shoulder, Troy smiled. "Yee-haw, Texas! Now that's what I'm talking about!" Troy waited for us at the top of the staircase. "I wondered where you two wandered off to, though I wouldn't worry about Aurora. She could kick your ass if you messed with her."

"I'm sure I would enjoy it," Gavyn said.

Most of the party-goers were gone. My watch told me it was midnight, and I was suddenly tired from my long day.

"Did you drive?" Gavyn asked.

"Nope, I took a cab."

"I'd like to give you a ride."

"I would like to take that ride.

He pulled me to him again, pressing his body into mine. "Is that so?"

I only smiled in response.

He threw a look at me with an unreadable expression.

Damn. Heat rushed my face. I hadn't meant it like that.

Well, maybe I had.

He led me to a sleek black car with dark tinted windows. It wasn't a luxury car by any stretch of the imagination.

"Where's your driver?"

"He was horrible. You know I got into a car accident?"

"Really? What a shame." I giggled and sank into the passenger seat while he held the door open for me.

"Okay, which way?" he asked once we pulled out of the maze of downtown one-way streets.

"Get on 1-10 West."

"Got it."

He drove well. Not too fast, not too slow. It made me wonder how well he did other things.

We were mostly silent for the trip, which ended up only taking a few minutes in the light traffic. As the car crawled past the gnarl of trees on my street, my nerves came to life.

"Are you all right over there? You look a little tense," Gavyn said. We glided into the parking lot.

"I'm good, thanks." I put my hand on the door, but I didn't leave.

He looked past me, out the window, and into the trees. "Does the tract of undeveloped land make you nervous?"

I took a deep breath and picked my swirling brain for a lie, but one wouldn't come. "Kind of. I was running the other morning and I saw someone hiding in the trees. It frightened me."

He furrowed his eyebrows, making a vertical line appear between his eyes. "Maybe it's a homeless person living out there. Please allow me to walk you to your door?"

"Sure, thanks."

I wasn't sure what his intentions were, not that mine were particularly innocent at the moment. I couldn't remember if I was wearing cute underwear or my regular stuff that came in a five pack from the discount store.

He opened my door for me, offering his hand to help me out. At his touch, my body buzzed with intentions to fly and burned with something else.

I stopped him outside my door. "This is me."

He tapped the metal numbers on my door, and then glanced behind him. "Hmm, first floor, facing the trees. Pretty, but not the safest for people living alone."

"Maybe you're right." I put my key in the door and pushed it open.

"Goodnight, Aurora." He kissed my forehead, embraced me, and then strode off without saying another word.

"Goodnight," I whispered to the dark, and then I went inside.

Chapter 4

"I'm melting!" Bree said. She flipped on her side and grabbed her phone. "According to my snazzy phone, it is currently ninety-four degrees, with sixty-nine percent humidity."

We were lying on a large blanket we'd spread on the edge of the soccer field near the law library. The solitary, large tree we were under provided some shade from the unforgiving sun.

"No wonder we're burning up, but it's nice to be outside." I flipped over on my stomach and rested my face on my folded arm. "Think about it. We're always in class or in the library studying. It gets old."

"Yes, but there is air conditioning. It's a wonderful thing."

I pulled the notepad between us closer to me. "Have we cracked this rule against perpetuities thing yet?" I stared at the flow chart we'd scribbled on the lined paper.

"I don't think we're meant to learn it. I think it's an old English common law nobody gives a shit about anymore, but we have to learn it because law school is the most backward thing ever."

I laughed. "I still don't see why learning this crap is going to translate into the real world, or help our understanding of modern real property law, for that matter."

"It's not. Whenever the professor starts a class by saying most students never get this down, then you know you're screwed." She shoved the notebook out of her line of vision. "Enough esoteric crap. Tell me about your party on Friday."

I flipped over on my back. The sky was a perfect bright blue, with a few puffy clouds floating around. "It was awesome."

"Did your guy show up?" she said.

"Yes, he did."

"And?"

I rolled over so we were facing again. "And I've been thinking about him all weekend, and today, and in every single class. It's kind of sad."

She wiggled her eyebrows. "Good stuff. Did you do it?"

"No, but we did hang out."

"You didn't do it? What else is there to do in a hotel on the freakin' Riverwalk?"

"Do you want to hear about it or not?"

"Okay. I'll keep my mouth shut for the next two minutes. Go."

"We walked around the Riverwalk and talked."

"About?"

"Everything. Anything. You know, books and other stuff."

"Seriously? Not sexy. We'll deal with it later. Continue."

I shot her a dirty look. "Well, he liked something because he kissed me, which was nice. Very, very nice."

"I hope there's more."

"Then he gave me a ride home and walked me to my door," I said.

"Well, did he call?"

"No. I was so out of it I forgot to give him my number, and he didn't ask. I'm so not slick."

She sat up, pulling me with her. "I think it's a good thing you didn't get his number and he doesn't have yours. Let him think about you for a couple more days. A little mystery goes a long way with men."

"I suppose. We'll see."

"What's his name? What does he look like?"

I hesitated. I wasn't sure how to protect his privacy. "His name is Gavyn. He's...tall, dark, and handsome."

My cell phone buzzed. Five text messages from my mom, all questioning whether I was still alive, why hadn't I called, etc.

I flipped my phone shut. "Hey, Bree. I better go. I need to call my mom. She's flipping out."

"Okay. I think I'm ready to go home anyways. My mascara is melting off my damn face."

I helped her fold up the blanket and draped it over her arms. "This was fun. I think I'll keep this in my trunk. See you later," she said.

I texted my mom back, assuring her I was alive, very busy, and fine.

It was a lie. I was afraid to run in the morning. I was afraid of the pecan grove. I was afraid because I could feel something watching me, even now.

The three story glass law school library flashed in the light as I approached. The late afternoon sun threw the corners of the building into shadows. As I walked past, I heard a soft click, and saw someone shift in the dark shadow of the building. The sidewalk was empty, but a mere fifty feet or so ahead, in the sunny courtyard, there were people.

"Is someone there?"

I waited for an answer that never came, then I gave up and strode into the sun.

෨ඏ

The next morning, I did something unusual. I actually paid attention to my appearance. Some of the girls wore cute, designer clothes to school every day. I assumed it was because they cared about their appearance and/or had extra money to spend on these types of things.

I was not one of those girls.

But today was different. If I was going to be miserable, I would at least look good doing it. I settled on a snug pencil skirt and fitted shirt with heels. The outfit hugged my curves, making me feel like a sexy pin-up girl.

I paused outside my door to make my silent, solemn, resolution. Today, I would not think or worry about Gavyn. I grabbed a banana and my purse and threw the front door open. After I'd locked it, I stood outside my apartment, digging through my purse to make sure my cell phone had made it inside.

A low, familiar chuckle startled me to attention. Gavyn was leaning against the wall outside my door, his arms folded across his chest. As soon as my eyes met his, he smiled. "Good morning."

I hugged him awkwardly, clutching a cell phone in one hand and a banana in the other. "Banana?" I pointed it at him.

"I'm good. Thanks." He gave me a wide, beaming smile. "May I give you a ride to school?"

"Sure."

He led me to his car, opened the passenger door and made a wide, sweeping gesture.

The early morning traffic was light so it only took a few minutes to get there. He parked on the edge of one of the parking lots attached to the law school, but left the engine idling. He leaned his head on the headrest. "Saturday and Sunday were crazy on set. I didn't have your phone number. I know Troy has it, but I wanted to get it from you myself. May I have it?"

"I suppose, since you already know where I live." I pulled a pen out of my purse and wrote my number on a scrap of paper. My hands were shaking and the numbers were jagged, but still legible. I handed it to him. He smiled and tucked it into his pocket. He drummed his fingers on the steering wheel, but made no move to shut off the engine.

He slid his right hand off the steering wheel, resting it on my bare knee. "I can't stop thinking about you." He leaned his head back on the headrest again, still looking at me. "At any rate, I just wanted to let you know."

I smiled, dropping my hand on top of his.

He seemed satisfied by my response. "Are you ready to go in?" he asked.

"Sure," I said.

We started the long walk to the entrance. He leaned close to me as we approached the sidewalk lining the edge of the campus. "I probably should keep this thought to myself, but you look ridiculously sexy today. Did you wear that to torture me?"

I cleared my throat to give my now mushy brain time to come up with a response. "Yeah, in the off chance you would show up outside my door without warning."

"Don't do that again," he spoke in my ear, his breath stirring the baby hairs on my neck. He paused at the junction of three sidewalks. One went to the law school, one went to the parking lot, and one went to the other side of campus. "I have two questions for you. Can you meet for lunch, and may I take you out for dinner tonight?"

"Maybe, if I get all my reading done, and yes."

"Okay. I'll take what I can get. I'll be at our Mexican place at 1:00 if you can make it." He brushed some stray hairs gently off my forehead before walking away.

Hot damn.

Once I made it to the classroom, I booted up my computer and pulled out my civil procedure book while I waited for Bree to arrive.

Gavyn's name floated through the room. My ears perked up.

Two girls were having a not so quiet conversation a couple of rows in front of me. "I saw him yesterday, can you believe it?" a blond I didn't know said in an extra loud voice.

"Oh, my God! I can't believe you saw Gavyn Dhaval. Where?" Liza asked. She had a strong, southern accent, shining black hair, and lots of money, judging by her the $8,000 bag she had one tanned arm draped over. As far as trust fund babies go, she was pretty darn nice.

"At the Alamo. They were filming a scene or something in the courtyard right there in front of everyone. Course, they had it blocked off so you couldn't walk up, but you could stand like twenty feet away." She brought the back of her hand to her forehead in a mock swoon. "He is super gorg! I wonder if he's single."

"I'm sure he would make himself single if he got a chance to meet you," Liza said in her sweet way. "I heard he was in the parking lot this morning with some girl."

"Shut up! Who told you?"

"Dean texted me. Said he saw him on his way in. Dean parks way out in the boonies because he's paranoid about his car getting a scratch."

"Oh, wow!"

Bree slid in next to me and powered up her laptop. "Phew. Almost late." She had a sheen of sweat on her forehead. "I had to hustle in from the parking lot."

Professor Tolane was busy locking the doors, which he did to ensure no latecomers came in. Of course, it counted as an absence, and he would flunk any student with more than four absences.

"What does he care if we are late? He still earns his one-hundred fifty grand regardless, and we still pay our $800 a freaking credit hour," I said.

"I care because being on time is so very important in the practice of law," Professor Tolane said.

Great. I managed to comment right when he was passing my desk to return to the front of the classroom to start class.

"Attention, future counselors of law. Ms. Lockette was just commenting on my late policy, which she appears to have a problem with. So, Ms. Lockette, what will you say to the judge when you run into a hearing ten minutes late? Please inform the class of your argument."

"I wouldn't be late to a hearing."

"Stand up please."

I did.

"Again, let us say you were late to a hearing or a trial. What would you say to the judge?"

I took a deep breath. "I would explain the reason for my delay and apologize."

"Uh huh. So, you would essentially say you were sorry?"

"Yes, I guess so."

"Sorry doesn't cut it. Sorry doesn't represent your client who is paying you to handle their legal affairs. Sorry won't get you out of the severe tongue lashing and order of contempt you will get from the judge. Sorry won't cover the legal consequences of your client losing a case because you didn't appear. And sorry will not cover the damage to your reputation as a careless attorney who doesn't respect a judge or litigant's time."

He lowered his glasses to stare at me. I wished I could melt into the floor and disappear from sight forever.

"You may be seated."

What an a-hole, Bree typed on her screen.

I think I hate law school, I typed back.

And I did.

࿇

At 12:50, I shoved my backpack into my locker before walking to the Mexican restaurant. It wasn't far, but I was kicking myself for wearing heels.

I managed to make it there a few minutes early. The parking lot was full of cars and the inside was packed with local workers. For lunch, the restaurant had a $4.00 all you can eat lunch buffet. I'd never seen a Mexican food buffet before, but it looked mighty tasty and I could actually afford it.

I was loading up my oval black plate when he appeared at my elbow.

"Fancy seeing you here," he murmured.

I dropped the serving spoon I was using to scoop the fruit salad onto my plate. It made a loud noise when it rolled off the table and hit the floor.

"Your skirt is ridiculous. It makes it hard for me to concentrate," he said.

I continued loading my plate with different foods, trying to appear nonchalant. "I'm glad you like it." I finally turned so I could see him, and damn, I'm glad I did. He was all movie star in a slick leather jacket and khakis. His normally unruly hair had been smoothed into obedience. It hung around his face, glossy and black. "You don't look so bad yourself."

We sat down at an empty table. "I only have fifteen minutes," he said, "so I have to eat fast."

"Go ahead and eat. I'm just glad I got to see you."

He looked up from his food with a serious face. "Is that so?"

"Yes."

He took a swig of water before he spoke again. "What are you in the mood for at dinner?"

"I pretty much like everything. Maybe Italian? But, you know, I'm open."

"I can handle that. Do you want to hit up a trendy place or are you more low key?"

"Low key. Like bottom floor low. I'm not one of the cool kids."

That made him smile. "Basement low it is. I'll be at your door at 7:30."

"Sweet."

We finished our food and stood to leave. "Aurora." He leaned close to me. I could smell his aftershave, which was very nice. "Don't wear your silly skirt tonight. It's very, very distracting and I'm trying to be gentleman."

Heat uncurled in my belly. I watched him leave the restaurant, all sinewy muscle and perfection.

Holy giant rhino balls.

I went back to school and sat through my classes, but the rest of the day merged into a big giant blur. Scary shadows forgotten, homework ignored. Finally, my last class let out. I tugged on Bree's arm while she was unloading her books into her trunk. She'd agreed to give me a ride home.

"Come on, let's go!"

"Simmer down, sweetheart. I'll get you home in time for your hot date." She yanked her hand away and swatted my hand. She shut the trunk and leaned against it. "I still can't believe he was waiting for you in the morning. I'd say it's eighty percent hot, twenty percent creepy."

"Hot. Not creepy." I grabbed her arm. "Let's go!"

She opened the driver's door while I jumped up and down outside the passenger door. "So, what are you wearing?"

That stopped me in my tracks. "Oh, crap! I have no idea. What should I wear?"

"Wear your tight aqua blue tank with your nice jeans. It will show off your toned shoulders and collarbone. Your butt is always a big hit in tight jeans."

"You're the best stylist ever!"

She flicked imaginary lint off her shirt. "I do what I can, young grasshopper."

As soon as she dropped me off, I ran into my apartment, stripped off my clothes, and jumped in the shower. I let the warm water run over my body. It calmed me down and made me feel whole again.

I put on the jeans and shirt Bree had suggested. The shirt did set off my shoulders nicely. It was fitted, but not tight. It skimmed over my bust, hinting at the fullness without showing any cleavage. I added some coral blue stone earrings and smiled at the effect.

I must admit, the blue made my skin look creamy and smooth and set off my eyes just right. I added a bit of eyeliner and mascara. I put on some lip-gloss and glanced at the clock. It was then I remembered my apartment was tiny and dingy, and right now it was a mess.

Crap. I darted around the small living room and picked up the clothes that had accumulated over the week. I dumped them into my closet before loading up my arms with coffee mugs and water glasses littering my table. I shoved my textbooks into one giant pile. It was a marginal improvement.

At precisely 7:30, there was a soft knock at my door. After one more look at my humble surroundings, I opened it. He was leaning against the doorframe, looking like he just stepped out of a high-fashion ad. His hair was disheveled and wild. He was wearing a t-shirt, a thin leather band around his wrist, and black jeans. His gaze roamed up and down my body before meeting my eyes.

He abruptly pushed past me and shut the door behind him. He grabbed my wrists and pulled me close to him. When our bodies collided, he dropped my wrists, put both of his hands on my face, and kissed me. His hands moved gently down my shoulders and arms then skimmed along the small of my back. He paused there, then wrapped his arms around my waist and pulled me tight, crushing me into his firm, muscular body.

This continued for a several seconds before he disentangled himself. "Sorry. I just couldn't help myself," he said. "I'll be a gentleman for the rest of the night. I promise." His finger traced the shape of my collarbone as he spoke. Heat rocked through my body, along with the familiar buzzing sensation, but I was in perfect control.

"Okay. Let's go." He held out his hand. We went out to his car with our fingers entwined. He weaved in and out of the San Antonio traffic, glancing at me as he drove.

"I should give you a heads up about something," he said. "It's kind of stupid and I hate to even mention it."

"What is it?"

"Sometimes when I go out in public, things will happen. Someone may come up and ask for an autograph, or sometimes photographers will show up."

"You mean, like the paparazzi?"

"Yeah. Sometimes employees of bars and restaurants will tip them off in exchange for cash. I try to stay off the radar and San Antonio is low key, so hopefully it won't happen. I don't want you to have to deal with it. You'll be safe with me though. I won't let them bother you."

"No biggee. I won't pick my nose or anything."

He smiled. "Thanks for being so cool about it. It's really embarrassing to even have to discuss this with you."

We pulled into a non-descript strip mall in a middle class neighborhood. He gestured at a small Italian restaurant in the far end of the mall. "It doesn't look like much, but it's really good food."

Booths and tables lined the walls. The lighting was dim. Greenery was everywhere, with ivy creeping up the walls. A massive wine rack dominated the front of the restaurant. Faint Italian opera music came through hidden speakers. The host immediately recognized Gavyn.

"Around the corner, sir?" he asked.

"Yes, please. Thank you," Gavyn replied.

He led us to a section of the restaurant out of view of the main door. Patrons gestured and whispered as we walked through.

There were only three small tables at the back section, all empty. "Let's keep this a private party," Gavyn said to the host, pressing a bill into his hand.

A discreet waiter took our food and wine order. We poured the wine and clinked our glasses together in a silent toast.

He watched me for a few minutes, not saying anything. For once, I did not feel the need to fill the silence that loomed between us.

"Aurora," he said. My heart jumped when I heard him say my name. "You really are beautiful."

"Oh, my God, don't start that again!"

"Quit deflecting my compliments. I've been all over the world, and believe it or not, people all start to look the same. But not you. There is something about your face. It's...lovely."

"Wow, thanks."

"Not to mention your figure," he said with a more devious smile.

"Watch it, mister." I pointed my finger at him.

He raised his hands in mock surrender. "Just sayin'. "

I smiled. "Okay. Duly noted. Can we talk about something else now? How does one go about becoming a famous movie star?"

"Dumb luck." He tapped the stem of his wine glass with his finger while he talked. "I was in theatre productions in London when I was a teenager. I liked acting, but I never actually thought I could turn it into a career, so I just did theatre in the summers for fun. A talent agent showed up at one of our modest productions and scouted me. I was filming my first major film six weeks later. The rest, you Americans would say, is history."

"It sounds like a little more than dumb luck. It sounds like you were picked out of a crowd."

"Just luck. It's not a bad life and I can't complain about the money, but it's been an adjustment. I can't go to a supermarket, or a shopping center, or to the movies, or to an airport without attracting some attention. I've enjoyed myself here. Not a lot of press, laid back culture, and there's this very special girl I've met."

His words moved through me. The rush of euphoria set my body ablaze with sensations. Some were very promising, some were scary, some were warning me I was on the edge of floating out my chair...literally. I began my slow count backwards from twenty, in my head.

He placed his hand on mine. "You okay?"

I smiled and glanced at our two hands touching on the table. "I am now."

The food, as promised, was excellent. By the end of the dinner, I was stuffed and a little tipsy. He paid the tab over my spirited objection and we walked out into the balmy night. As soon as we moved outside, his face changed. He put his arm over my shoulder and pulled me close to him. "Walk fast. Sorry."

"What's wrong?" I followed his gaze to the cluster of photographers across the street. "Oh."

"You're not upset?"

"They'll crop me out of the picture anyways."

He laughed louder and rubbed my shoulder as we walked to the car. "I was planning on taking you to a wine bar, but do you mind if we go back to my hotel and hang out?"

"Not at all." I pushed back the stream of dirty thoughts popping into my head at the prospect of being alone with him in a hotel room.

He flashed me his bright smile as we got in the car. He peeled out of the parking lot and whizzed down a couple of side streets before making his way back to the hotel. He pulled in the front of a ritzy hotel downtown. A valet appeared and took the car while Gavyn ushered me inside. The bronze elevator doors slid open as we approached. He pushed the button for the twenty-sixth floor. I waggled my eyebrows at him. "Oohh. The penthouse."

I was joking, but of course, it turned out to be the penthouse suite. There was a distinct living room with a couch, recliner, and a huge flat screen. The king-size bed was on a raised platform off to the side. I peeked in the bathroom. It had a large Jacuzzi and a separate walk-in shower. "Wow. Penthouse was right on the mark. Nice!"

"Yeah, it's included in my contract." He waived his hand at the television. "You want to watch a movie?"

"Sounds nice."

We settled on a thriller. I sat down on the couch a couple of feet from him as the movie started. He chuckled and wrapped his arms around me, pulling me close to him until I was sitting on his lap. "What are you doing all the way over there?"

I settled in next to him and leaned my head against his broad shoulder. He wrapped his arms around me.

I woke up in the dark. The movie credits were scrolling down the screen as a heavy metal song played in the background.

I was still on the couch with Gavyn. He was asleep against the arm of the couch. I gave myself a minute to admire his handsome features. It was late, and I had to be up in a few hours. I had no idea what time he needed to be up.

I shut off the giant television then pushed his legs further on to the couch. I pulled a blanket off the top of the bed and returned to the couch to spread it over him.

I called the front desk. By the time I made it downstairs, a cab was waiting for me. I spent the cab ride trying to count backwards from twenty to control my body, but my mind always returned to Gavyn. As the car turned onto my street and drove past the forest, I didn't feel any fear, nor a sensation of being watched. It was a normal, quiet forest, and for the moment, I was a normal girl.

Chapter 5

I yawned my way through my early morning class. I was tired, and worse, I was bored because Bree hadn't shown up. Finally, the professor released us from his never-ending drone.

A little envelope on my phone alerted me to a voice mail. My heart jumped at the little spark of hope it was him.

"Hey, Aurora. It's me. I just thought I would test your number. I was very disappointed to wake up without you, but I'm glad we hung out last night. I'm guessing you're in class. I just got my call sheet and I will be out of pocket for the next couple of days with filming. I didn't want you to think I was ignoring you. I'll be thinking of you. Okay. Bye."

I hung up and sunk into one of the chairs in the courtyard. Images of tall, dark, and handsome filled my head.

"You liar! How could you not tell me?" I looked up. All five feet one inches of Bree were standing in front of me. Her hands were on her hips, and she looked pissed. Really pissed.

"What?"

"I can't believe you! You didn't tell me you were dating Gavyn Dhaval! How could you leave that out?" She slammed her purse down before dropping into one of the chairs at the table. "Seriously, how could not tell me?"

"Dude, lower your voice. How did you find out?"

"Not from you for damn sure." She leaned forward in her chair. "I saw it on the internet. There's a picture of you two on one of the blogs I read."

"Oh, crap." I hid my face in my hands. "I don't want that kind of attention, and I don't think he does either."

She pulled down one of my hands so she could see my face. "Hey, relax. It's on a blog, not a tabloid." She smiled. "They called you the mystery woman."

I sunk my head on the table and groaned. "No, no, no. Not good. Please kill me now."

She laughed. "Oh, stop. It's freaking awesome you're dating a movie star. You have a lot of surprises, don't you?" She patted my arm. "I knew you had a big secret." She shook her head. "I knew it."

"Well, shit. Cat's out of the bag," I said.

"Don't worry too much. I doubt very many people read that particular blog."

But we glanced around us to find the eyes of several of my classmates resting definitively on me. Their whispers filled the air.

"Or I could be wrong," Bree added.

"Great." I grabbed my backpack. "I'm going to go to the gym."

"Stay here with me. I want to hear more about him."

"I'm sorry. I can't deal with this right now. Thanks for the offer though."

As soon as I rounded the corner of the administrative building, a cold, hard feeling nestled at the base of my spine.

It was here. I could feel it.

I picked up my pace as I passed the tree grove. It was a bright, nearly cloudless day, but there were lots of shadows, way more than the trees would create.

They were out there.

Reaction flowed through me and before I could stop it, my feet were off the ground a few inches.

"Crap!"

I sank back down to the ground and looked around. Thankfully nobody was around to see my freak show, but I had more pressing problems. A dark figure had emerged from the trees.

I ran until my backpack ripped and my books went flying all over the place. I stopped to pick them up. I was far away from the tree grove and I didn't see any shadows. Students gave me funny looks as I cried and shoved my books into my broken backpack.

When I finally had my books contained, I sat on the nearest bench, far from any tree groves. Young undergrads were milling around a nearby coffee stand with their lattes, no doubt worried about first dates, English 101, and their roommates.

I pondered the only two possibilities I could think of. The first one, and the most likely, was me losing my mind.

Second, and far more dangerous, was what I saw was real.

My cell phone buzzed in my pocket.

"Hello?"

"We need to talk."

"Mom, now is not really a good time," I said.

"What are you doing carrying on with a movie star? Are you crazy?" She continued as if I hadn't said a word. "My friend forwarded me some celebrity gossip blog, and behold there you were in a recent paparazzi photograph with Gavyn Dhaval."

"Mom, I—"

"A Hollywood actor? Do you realize how many fans he's probably had sex with?"

"It's really not like that."

"Sure. They all seem nice at first, but don't be naïve. All men are like that."

"Mom, really?" I shoved my broken backpack on the ground. "I'm an adult, and we are not having this conversation right now."

"Oh, yes we are. He's famous. If it happens in front of him..."

"I'm the one who can fly here, okay? I'm painfully aware of the risk. End of discussion."

"Ah." She was quiet on the other end of the line for a while. "I knew this would happen someday. I knew you would fall in love, and this would come up."

"Whoa, whoa whoa. There's no L word being thrown around here."

"I know my own child. I should be happy for you, but I'm just too worried."

"I'll be very careful around him, okay?"

"If you truly fall in love with a man, it's going to be very difficult to keep any part of yourself from him."

I picked up my mangled backpack. "We're not there yet. I'm definitely not there yet and I'm not getting into this right now with you. I need to go."

"Fine, just tell me one thing."

"What is it?" I asked.

"Are you on the pill?"

"Mom, oh my God! We are not talking about this, okay?"

"If you are sexually active you should—"

"Yes, okay? Stop, now. For the love of all that is holy."

After I hung up the phone, I cried. When I was done, I walked out to my car and drove home.

⤲⤲

I stayed home for two days on a claim of sickness. Gavyn didn't call, but I knew he wouldn't with his schedule.

After a couple of afternoons of daytime television, I was bored enough to go back to school. Bree was happy to see me, and I must admit, it was nice to return to some sort of normalcy.

I sat with her in the courtyard after our second class. She was filling me in on her latest date, and nobody was staring at me.

That didn't last long.

"Hi, ladies." Gavyn appeared out of nowhere. "Mind if I join you?" He sat down next to me, across from Bree.

As usual, he wore big sunglasses and a baseball cap, but it was still obvious it was him. He extended a hand to Bree. "You must be Bree. I'm Gavyn."

54

She shook his hand without hesitation. "Very nice to meet you," she said, as if she met movie stars every day.

Other people were not so calm. Students stared openly. The courtyard filled up as more and more people found a reason to come outside.

"Hey, babe." He kissed my hand.

I saw several female classmates giving me looks ranging from envy to admiration. I did my level best not to look too smug.

Okay, maybe I didn't try at all.

"Hey," I said.

"I'm on a quick break. We're filming at the church on campus today, but do you want to have dinner tonight?" He lowered his voice to a whisper. "Something low key. I guess our little outing got picked up on the tabloid circuit. I'm very sorry."

"I'm sorry you were photographed with me. It's probably not good for your career."

Bree chimed in. "Not true. You look super hot in the photos."

Gavyn smiled at her. "I agree with Ms. Bree here. You looked amazing." He returned his attention to me. "Really. I didn't want you to have to deal with this."

"This is small potatoes. So, what time should I come over tonight and what should I bring?"

"Whenever you get back from school. I'll order in some food for dinner. The only thing you need to bring is yourself." He smiled, but it wasn't his normal smile. It looked a little strained.

"Okay. Consider it done."

He stood. "Awesome, I better go." He glanced around at the growing mass of students. "It's getting a little crowded here. Nice to meet you, Bree."

And then he was gone, his bodyguards surrounding him the second he stepped away from the table.

I dropped my head against the back of my chair. "Oh, swoon!"

Bree giggled. "Oh, my God, he is positively dreamy. And so nice and normal."

"I know."

"Have you guys done it yet?" she asked.

I lifted my head. "You and your dirty mouth."

"You need to use your dirty mouth on him. That man is sexual perfection," she said.

I agreed.

Three hours later, I was freshly showered, clad in jeans and a low-cut fitted shirt that did nothing to hide my bust, and standing outside the penthouse suite.

"Good. You're here," he said, giving me a quick hug as he opened the door. "I just ordered some food. I had a feeling you would get here around this time."

I walked into his giant room. It appeared he had done some tidying up since the last time I was here. He walked up behind me and wrapped his arms around me. "How is it you make jeans look sexy?"

"I'm glad you think so because I'm definitely a t-shirt and jeans girl.

"One more thing to love about you," he said. My heart jumped at the word.

A white-capped service attendant delivered the champagne, prime rib and steamed vegetables, set them on the small two-top near the window, and left quickly.

"Have you ever had a serious relationship?" he asked after our champagne toast.

I gulped it down. "Abrupt topic change much?"

"Well?"

"Not really."

"Really? You're twenty-three and you've never been in a serious relationship?"

"No."

"May I ask, why not?" he asked with his super sexy smile.

"Just haven't met the right person, I suppose." I shrugged, hoping he couldn't read the lie in my eyes.

"Hmm. Aren't you going to ask me the same question?"

"No. It doesn't have any relevance to today and now."

I pushed my plate away, walked over to him and stood in front of him. He scooted his chair away from the table, confused. He started to rise, but I put my hand down on his chest, gently pushing him back in the chair.

I straddled him. He looked surprised, but smiled as I leaned forward and kissed him.

His hands slid down my back and parked in my back pockets. I ran my fingers through his thick and unruly hair. When I did, he turned his face up to me. His mouth tasted sweet and warm. His hands left my pockets as he brought them to my face, then through my hair, finally moving them so he was cradling my neck.

I took a deep breath and pulled away. He leaned back in his chair and exhaled as his hands fell to his sides. "Something wrong? Sorry if I—"

"I'm the one who jumped on your lap, remember?"

"You must really like beef," he said, gesturing at our plates. "If I had any idea you would react this way, I would have taken you to steakhouse the first time we met."

He pulled me back into his arms, dissolving all my concerns when his warm lips touched mine. The buzzing filled my body, and I was in trouble. For a brief moment, only his arms were keeping me on the chair.

His eyes flew open. "Are you okay? Did I do something wrong?"

He hadn't seen anything and I was now firmly planted on the chair. I tried to give him a reassuring smile. "I just couldn't catch my breath there. I'm sorry. You can do that whenever you like."

"For a split second, you felt weightless in my arms." He rubbed his temples with his eyes closed. "I'm so sleep deprived it's not even funny."

Shit. Super, stinky, double triple shit. "Um, bathroom." I stood.

"What?" He dropped his hands from his face. "You okay?"

"Yep, just need to go. Excuse me." I fled the room.

I put my hands on either side of the sink and faced myself in the mirror. It was time for a reality check.

He was going to find out. It was only a matter of time before I lost it in front of him. I should make an excuse, walk out the door, and never see him again.

Even as I thought it, I knew I wouldn't do it. There was something with him I could not walk away from.

Bad decision, I knew. But it was done.

I returned to him. He looked at me with tense eyes.

"Where were we?" I asked.

"You okay?"

"Yes. Are you?"

He took my hand and led me to his bed, sitting on the edge. "I'm sorry. I'm so exhausted. I can't even function any more."

I sat next to him. "I'll get out of your hair so you can sleep."

"Stay," he whispered. "No funny business. I promise. I never thought I would say this, but I would rather sleep than do anything else."

I did, wearing his boxers and t-shirt, snuggled against his chest.

Chapter 6

"Clean up in aisle three, cleanup in aisle three." The annoying old-school twang was clear in the announcer's voice. I was standing in front of the canned goods, thinking about dirty things I wanted to do to Gavyn instead of looking for the low-sodium canned green beans on my list.

I'd spent the night in bed with him and had the cute note he'd left on my pillow in the morning snug in my left pocket to prove it. He'd fallen asleep right away, but that didn't stop me from thinking about it and him all night.

I glanced to my right. A very wiry man with hair so blond it was almost white stood near the end of the aisle. I wondered, for an instant, if he could tell what I was thinking. Of course not.

I grabbed the green beans and shoved them into my cart. I normally enjoyed grocery shopping, but it was much more difficult with Troy's restrictions and my restricted budget. Too bad I was the only one who saw the results of my hard work. Soon, though, maybe not. More dirty thoughts paraded through my mind.

I finished my grocery shopping and dropped them off at my apartment. I'd hurried to my door without a glance at the trees. I felt the darkness, but I ignored it and kept walking with my head held high. It was my new tactic: ignore bad things and maybe they will go away.

My next stop was the bookstore. It was high time I bought some reading material that didn't involve torts, the Uniform Commercial Code, or obscure English common law.

I parked in the parking lot of the largest bookstore in town. It was tucked into the side of an uppity open air shopping mall. It was a glossy, national chain store with huge floor to ceiling windows expanding to the second floor.

I perused the fiction section. I loved everything about books from the way they smelled to the little worlds contained between their pages. Passing through the sci-fi section, white-blond hair caught my eye.

It was distinct, that platinum hair color. I'd seen it before, today actually, at the grocery store.

He shifted as he re-shelved his book. It gave me a chance to glimpse his features in profile. It was him.

I was being followed outright now. No trees needed.

I put the book I was holding down with a shaky hand. In a city of over a million, what were the chances?

The familiar buzzing sensation went through my body as I went on high alert. I slowly walked out from the tall row of books. I ducked behind a display shelf of new releases lining the second floor until I was near the escalator. I stepped onto it and waited to go down, not wanting to even make the noise of walking down the metal surface.

As I descended to the first floor, I watched him. He glanced in the direction of where I'd been standing, and then scanned the second floor with a little anxiety in his face. When he saw me descending, relief washed over his features.

That was the look he left me with.

As soon as I got to the first floor, I dumped my selections on a nearby shelf, and took off like a rocket out the front door. I almost ran into a woman with bright curly red hair. "Pardon me," I croaked as I shouldered past her and into the sunlight.

Once I was back in my car, I hit the major loop around the city and went north, instead of south, which was the way home.

I tried to make note of the tiny cars in my rearview mirror like I saw in detective movies, but in the late afternoon traffic it just wasn't practical and I didn't think my junkmobile would survive another fender bender.

I got home just as the sun was descending behind the hills in the north. The presence in the trees was quiet, but definitely there.

I bolted my door, and put the chair back up against it. I checked my cell phone to make sure it had a full signal and dug pepper spray out of the recesses of my purse and set it on the table.

I sat on the couch and stared at the black television screen. I couldn't tell my mom because she would freak out, and I didn't want to go home and have whatever was going on follow me to her house. That left me with no one to tell. I was trapped, alone in my head.

At some point, I would have to take action instead of pretending weird things were not happening to me, but not today.

I poured a large glass of wine and pulled out my school reading assignment for the following Monday. Thank God it was Friday. Maybe if I got drunk enough tonight, I could sleep away at least part of the weekend.

୬‿୧

The ringing of my cell phone woke me up the next morning. I answered without looking at the caller I.D.

"Yeah?"

"Will you let me in please?" Gavyn's voice came over the line.

I was shocked out of my sleepy state. "Oh! Yeah, just a sec."

I hung up the phone and darted out of bed toward the bathroom. A quick glance in the mirror confirmed I looked like absolute crap. I brushed my hair, used mouthwash, and splashed my face with water. Thank God my nightgown was short and cute. I glanced in the mirror again. There was marginal improvement, but I still looked pretty bad.

I opened the door and he strode right in. He was wearing khakis and a snug t-shirt, which hugged his broad shoulders. He had the usual leather strap around his wrist. Even though I had spent a lot of time with him, his obnoxiously perfect good looks always caught me by surprise. "Good morning. I've been knocking at your door for a few minutes, but I figured you were asleep." He appraised me. "You look cute."

"No, I don't." I looked down at my rumpled gown. "What time is it?"

"10:00 a.m. and our lunch reservations are at 12:00. I'll wait while you get ready." He plopped down on my couch. He removed the empty wineglass from the top of a pile of books, picked one up, and flipped through it. I stared at him for a few seconds before I understood he wasn't going to leave.

I did my best to focus on a hot shower and brushing my teeth, trying not to think of the gorgeous man sitting ten feet away in the living room.

I stepped out of the shower dripping wet, wrapped a towel around me securely, and walked out of the bathroom. "What should I wear? What kind of place is this?"

He dropped the book he was holding. "How am I supposed to answer your questions when you look like that?" His British accent was stronger than normal.

I followed his eyes as they roamed over my body. My wet towel was white, and now see through. Not a lot left to the imagination.

Oops.

I stood in front of him, fiery tension working its way through my body as he watched me with desperate, hungry, eyes.

I cleared my throat. "Dress it is." I forced myself to step away from him. I would not jump his bones like a cat in heat. Nope. Not me.

I came out of the bathroom in my sundress, towel drying my hair.

Gavyn was waiting for me right outside the bathroom door. He swept me up and carried me to the bed, gently laying me down. He lay on top of me, propping himself up with his arms to keep his full weight off of me.

"What were you saying?" His hand went up my dress, gently caressing the outside of my thigh. His fingertips danced down my leg and rested around my knee.

With one strong motion, he pulled my knee up, wrapping my leg around his torso. His hardness pressed into me. My breath hitched as I pushed back into him.

His soft lips traveled down my neck, into the hollow of my throat. He moved my sundress strap with his fingertip, stroking my skin as he did so. His mouth traveled oh so gently across my collarbone.

I writhed under him, desperate to taste him, to touch him.

He entwined his hands with mine and pushed them to either side of my head. His lips were on my hungry mouth.

My body exploded with a hollow, thirsty longing for him. I wrapped my other leg around him, and arched my back.

"Stop being such a gentleman, please," I breathed, tugging at the bottom of his shirt and pulling it over his head, admiring his finely muscled shoulders and torso.

"As you wish," he said, eyes burning.

He pushed himself into me, strong hands roaming my body. My sundress fluttered to the floor, followed quickly by my bra and panties.

His mouth was hot on mine, our bodies wrapped together in heaving flesh on flesh. We moved together, travelling higher and higher with a rough abandon. Then I was soaring, and I was his, and he was mine.

He yelled my name as I contracted around him.

I collapsed next to him. My thoughts scattered in a thousand different directions as my body hummed with pleasure.

"Wow," he said.

"Wow," I agreed.

We lay in bed for several minutes until our breathing slowed. He propped himself on one elbow and absently traced circles on my stomach with his finger.

I giggled and pulled up the sheet.

"No," he said, pushing it back. "Please let me enjoy the view."

I rolled so I was facing him. "I'm starving."

"Oh, but I'm not done." His hands slid down my body to a place where they were much appreciated.

Eventually hunger overtook other urges.

I bounded out of bed, pulling my sundress on in record time. I tried to get a handle on my messy but mostly dry hair. By the time I was done, Gavyn was already dressed and waiting. "Ready?"

"Yep. Where are we going anyways?"

"It's a surprise."

We walked into the parking lot, but he led me over to a midnight blue luxury car.

"New ride?" I asked.

"It's safer and,"—he bent down to whisper in my ear—"a little sexier, no?"

"That,"—I turned my lips into his—"it is."

I settled into my seat and watched the pretty hill-country terrain fly by. The Guadalupe River ran by the road. Through the trees, the sun danced off the swiftly moving water.

We stopped in front of massive, Victorian style home nestled against thick trees. Fountains dotted the huge front yard. Multi-colored pebbled stones curved a walkway to the front porch. Graceful white columns towered on the front of the house. It was three floors, all bright sparkling white.

"Bed and breakfast?" I said.

"Yes. You like?"

"Haven't you had enough today, young man?"

He helped me out of the car. "No, but we're not getting a room here."

Gavyn grabbed my hand and pulled me through the lobby and out a rear exit. Outside, a beautiful restaurant was built onto a large deck. Small round tables with white table clothes shifting in the breeze filled the space. Each table was topped by a bright aqua colored umbrella. It was perfect, and very private.

He was watching me as we sat down. "This is beautiful," I told him. "Really. This is perfect."

"Good. I hoped you would like it," he said.

The waiter brought over the menus. A single dish cost more than I spent on groceries in a week. Reflexively, I started scanning for the lowest priced items.

Gavyn was watching me closely. "Do you not like French food?"

I laughed. Sometimes I forgot we lived in different financial stratospheres. "No, the prices. Sticker shock."

"My treat. Please order whatever you'd like."

"Thanks. I appreciate it, but that's not what I'm worried about."

"Then?"

"It's these places I couldn't otherwise afford without you footing the bill all the time. I'm not entirely comfortable with it. I'd like to be able to pay for some stuff, too."

"I understand. But if I take my girlfriend out to a nice lunch, I want you to be able to accept it. I've never had anyone to share this with."

"Okay, but within reason, and you know, it won't hurt us to eat at normal people restaurants every once in a while."

He smiled. "As opposed to abnormal people restaurants?"

I snapped my menu shut. "Correct."

After a delectable lunch where I discovered I love things drenched with truffle oil, he drove to a small town nearby with a huge farmer's market. I walked around the stalls, admiring the different cultural crafts, the brightly colored fruits and vegetables, and the wide variety of people. Soon, every direction I looked someone was snapping pictures of Gavyn as he walked by.

When a definitive crowd formed around us, he put his fingers on his brow, blocking his face with his hand. "Let's go. Sorry."

"Don't apologize."

By the time we got back to his hotel, the sunlight was fading behind the hills in the distance.

As soon as he shut the door behind me, he pulled my sundress over my head and carried me back to the bed. After some spirited adult activities, we were a sleepy, happy tangle in the soft bed. As sleep overcame me, I decided this was the best day of my life.

So far.

Chapter 7

I took my time parking in the crisp, fall morning. The semester was creeping to a close. It should've been a relief, but it wasn't. Finals were coming up. Since one final was one hundred percent of your grade for a class, it tended to add some stress to your life.

I got out of the car and mashed the buttons on the electronic key until it beeped twice. I was eighty percent sure that meant the car was locked now.

"That isn't your car," said a feminine voice directly behind me.

"Jesus Christ, Bree! Don't sneak up on me."

She smiled. "This must be Gavyn's, unless you've been pretending to be poor this entire time."

"He leases it, and yes, he added my name to the lease." I pushed some buttons again until the trunk popped open.

She fished my backpack out and handed it to me. "That's pretty significant, don't you think?"

I shrugged.

We walked through the parking lot together. "I guess I shouldn't be surprised. You practically live with him," she said.

"Not true."

"Oh yeah? When was the last time you slept in your own apartment?"

"Hmm. I suppose it's been a few weeks." I hooked my arm through hers as we approached the classroom building. "Do you blame me?"

"That I do not."

My classmates were nice enough not to stare at me anymore for dating a movie star. One of my other classmates was dating a professional basketball player. I was glad for the focus to slide to her.

"I like you better when you're getting laid. You're a lot more relaxed. I guess you just needed some orgasms to get those endorphins flowing," Bree said.

"You're all sorts of wrong, you know?"

She wiggled her hips in her special dork dance. "Actually, I'm the shiz. Speaking of which, you know about the par-tay this weekend, right?"

"Nope." I opened the doors to the building and gestured for her to walk in front of me.

"Of course, you've been constantly holed up in your luxury suite with Gavyn. It's a law school tradition. Every Halloween weekend, everybody drives up to the Guadalupe River in the hill country. The student bar association rents out cabins and campgrounds. We party, hike, eat, drink and play for the weekend. Families and significant others are included."

"Cool. You going?" Hill country meant thick, tall trees. Lots of trees gave strange people places to hide and stalk me, but I hadn't seen anyone in a while. Probably because I spent most of my free time in Gavyn's bed.

"Girl, shoot! Hell to the yes I'm going, and so are you."

"Well, maybe I could go for one night."

"What? Go for two, with me. Bring Gavyn. It'll be fun."

"I don't know," I said.

"Oh, come on. People have gotten used to the idea of him being your boyfriend, or whatever he is. I bet after a few hours people would stop staring. I'll spread the word for people to treat him like everyone else. No autographs or anything."

"We'll see. I'll talk to him."

She grabbed my arm outside the classroom door. "You need to do this. These classmates are going to be your coworkers someday. It is a very small legal community, and you need to try, at least a little bit." She let go of my arm and opened the door for me. Her bright smile was back. "Plus, I'm going. And you know you love me, bee-yotch."

"Okay, okay."

ॐॐ

After a long day of classes and library study time, I drove home to find Gavyn stretched out on my couch and flipping through channels. His presence shouldn't be a surprise to me since I'd given him a key, but he never ceased to knock my socks off with his general hotness.

"Hello, my lady." He pulled me into a tight embrace.

"Hi."

He kissed the tip of my nose. "Did you finish all your reading?" he asked.

"Yes. What time did you get up this morning?" He'd been gone when I woke up at 5:30.

"3:00," he said. "It did not feel good, but I had to be there by 3:30."

"You must be tired." I threw my backpack on the ground near the front door and lowered myself on to the couch.

He sat next to me. He looked tired, pale, and his eyes were off. "You want to go to the wine bar?"

We ordered a Chilean red and found a small couch in the corner of the dimly lit bar.

He looked at me for a couple of minutes without saying a word. He was fidgety, playing with the leather strap on his wrist and continually adjusting his shirt.

"Something wrong?" I asked.

"No, not wrong. Not really." He stuttered when he spoke. It was weird. He never stuttered. Stuttering was my gig.

"What is it?"

He ran both of his hands though his thick black hair, still not saying a word. He took the wine glass out my hand and set it on the table, wrapping his hand around mine.

Oh crap. I was so getting dumped.

"Aurora." His voice was very quiet. "I love you." He took a deep, shaky breath before continuing. "I'm sorry if this is too soon."

Whoa. My heart flip-flopped around in my chest. Crap. Wait, this was good. And bad. And Complicated.

But I did.

He held up a hand. "You don't have to say anything if you're not ready. Are you okay with this?"

"Yes, because I love you," I said, testing the words in my mouth. They felt good.

He cradled my face in his hands and kissed me. "Thanks."

"Thanks?" I repeated. "Why are you thanking me?"

"For being you. And loving me."

"Now that we are officially lovers, do you have free time this weekend?" I asked.

"Yes. Why?" His face was dark again.

"It's a law school thing, a tradition on Halloween weekend where the student bar association rents out some cabins on the Guadalupe River in the hill country. People bring their families or whatever, camp out, and have a good time. Bree wants me to go, and she thinks you should go too."

"Would you like me to go with you?"

I took a long drink of my wine. "Yes. I don't want to be away from you the whole weekend."

He looked at his hands, which were folded on the table. "Okay. I'll go."

"What's wrong? You don't have to go if you don't want to."

"We're wrapping production down here next week. I'm going back to L.A."

"Oh." Now it was my turn to stare at my lap.

"Please say something," he said.

"That blows."

He smiled, but it was weak and didn't reach his eyes. "I'm going to figure something out." He reached for my hand. I hesitated, but he grabbed it and squeezed it between his. "I mean it when I say I love you. I want this. I want you. I will figure this out for us, okay?"

"Okay. Sure." I tried to smile back, but I could already feel the slices of pain about his impending departure.

��

Gavyn drove to the campground on the Guadalupe. South Texas had blessed us with perfect seventy-eight degree weather and a cloudless blue sky. It was only a forty-five minute drive from downtown, but we were both silent. It felt like we were driving to a funeral. After all, it was our last weekend together.

The silence was okay. I needed some time to think.

I had let myself fall in love. Time to cue the happy music and ride off into the sunset.

Reality was a little different. Gavyn was based out of London and Los Angeles. He was a movie star with a very tight schedule that would pull him all over the world. I was a poor law student in Texas, with a demanding schedule that would tether me to my law school. More importantly, I was a circus freak. There was no way I'd be able to hide it from him forever.

But there was a tiny little piece of good in all this. If Gavyn lived in Los Angeles and I lived in San Antonio, then maybe I could hide it from him. I'd just have to exercise great caution for the next few dates and the time we spent together in the future. At least I could buy some time to figure out if Gavyn had a permanent relationship in mind, something that would warrant a full disclosure of all superhuman attributes.

"Hey, beautiful, glad to see you're smiling."

"Thanks. I'm happy to be with you right now."

"Good." He reached over to pat my leg. "I hope you don't mind. I got us a little private cabin."

"Oh?"

Of course, it turned out it was no simple cabin. It was two stories, with a loft overlooking the living room, and a vaulted ceiling with a skylight. There was a full kitchen with stainless steel appliances, stately leather furniture, and huge bedroom with the biggest bed I had ever seen. A small back patio, complete with rocking chairs, overlooked a beautiful view of trees and a sliver of bubbling river. The cabin was at least five times the size of my apartment.

"Gavyn! This isn't a freaking cabin. This is a house!"

"Do you like it?"

"Oh, my God! It's too much."

"It's really not a big deal for me to do this, so let me do it, okay?"

"Right, sure." I nodded.

"What time did you say the barbeque was?" he asked.

"Three. What did you have in mind?"

He maneuvered me onto the ridiculously large bed and showed me what he had in mind.

We managed to crawl out of bed and get dressed by mid afternoon. I was sore in the right places and my legs were shaky, but Gavyn was a ball of energy. He loaded up a small backpack cooler with our steaks, beer, and ice.

"You ready?" His smile was so wide it looked like his face might split open.

"Yeah."

"I was thinking we could walk. It's not even a mile away, and it's so nice outside. We'll walk back and get our car before it gets dark," he said.

"Good idea."

He pulled a map out of his packet, consulted it, and seemed confident with what he saw. He led me to the thick tree line right behind the cabin.

The trail we chose was a narrow strip of packed dirt. Knobby tree roots stretched across the path, which I, in my infinite grace, occasionally stumbled over. Gavyn kept his hand on my arm during the steep parts, making sure I wouldn't fall. The trees were so thick that only small streams of sunlight filtered through the leaves, making woven patterns on the ground. Occasionally, we would hear rustling in the trees as we approached and scattered the wildlife.

At first, I was uncomfortable with the deafening silence of the forest. When my ears adjusted to the quiet, I could hear the birds chirping, insects buzzing, the creaking of the tops of the trees as they swayed in the wind, and the occasional dim roar of a nearby river.

We came across three picnic tables in the shade of a large tree, barely visible from the trail. A small brook bubbled nearby. We sat down at the small picnic table, brushing off as much vegetation as we could.

Gavyn met my eyes. "I have a little surprise for you."

"You do?"

"It's something I made for you during my down time on set. No big deal." He pulled something small and brown out of his pocket. It was a narrow leather bracelet similar to the one he wore. It was made of tiny strings of leather, woven together. The braid of the weave was dotted with small pearly sea-shells.

"It's beautiful. I love it. Thank you." I leaned across the table and gave him a loud smack on the lips.

"I'm glad you like it." He tied the bracelet on.

I held out my arm and admired it again. "One of a kind."

"Yes, you are." His face became more serious. "I want to talk to you about something. Something important."

I got up from my position across from him, and sat next to him, straddling the bench so I could face him. "Okay."

"I've been thinking about us a lot. I know I'm hard to be with. I'm contractually obligated for about the next two and half years with various projects."

I nodded, since I already knew about his upcoming projects.

"And you. You and your brilliant little brain are in law school." He shifted his body so he was facing me. "Let me ask you something. If you could do anything you want, without regards to consequences, what would you do?"

"No one has ever asked me before. I'm not sure I've asked myself before."

"I'm asking you now." He nudged me with his shoulder. "I know you space out a lot, so what are you thinking about?"

"Mostly you."

"Seriously, what do you want to do?"

"I really don't know what I want to do with myself on a permanent basis, if that's what you're asking. I hate law school. I think it was a mistake." I dropped my eyes to my lap. I had never admitted that out loud, or even to myself for that matter.

He took my hand. "Well, then my plan might be perfect."

At this point, my nerves had taken me to a point where I was pretty sure I would throw up if I opened my mouth to speak, so I kept it shut and waited for him to elaborate.

"I love you. You know that." He squeezed my hand. "I want to be with you. I can't imagine my life without you. I want us to grow old together. I don't know how you feel about marriage, but that's where I'm headed with this. I'm serious about you.

I've been turning our situation over and over in my mind. I'm willing to do whatever it takes to be with you. I'll make any sacrifice. I'll do whatever you ask of me.

I can't stand the thought of us living in two different cities. I don't want to be apart from you. I'm going to ask you something, and you can say no. I'm selfish to even ask. Please don't be angry with me, because I have Plan B, and a Plan C in case you don't like this one."

He stroked my face with his thumb. "Just be with me. You do anything you want. I want you to come with me on press tours, come with me when I shoot on location. I know it's selfish to ask you to leave your life and live mine. After I'm done with all the contracts I've already signed, I can live wherever you want. You can go to school, buy a house, do whatever you want. It would be 100% what you want to do."

I tried to wrap my mind around what he was offering me. "I can't just let you take care of me. That's not right."

"Do you have any idea how much money I have? I respect your independence. All I'm asking is for you to be with me. All of me. Even the part of me with a lot of money." He crossed his arms. "I have forty million dollars sitting in the bank, with plenty more coming."

"Jesus Christ. Your tax bill must be insane."

He gave me a small smile. "Seriously. What do you think of my plan?"

"It sounds like heaven, but I have some very serious reservations about letting you take care of me financially. I know you have a lot of money, but I don't want to be 'that' girl. You know?" I stood. "I need a moment."

We returned to the trail, walking in silence for several minutes. I could feel him watching me, no doubt trying to figure out all the emotions flickering across my face. The roar of the river was getting louder, and the faint sounds of a boom-box and crowds of people were flitting through the trees.

As soon as he asked, I knew I was going to say yes and start my new life. I also knew I would have to tell him about it. I made a decision. Tonight I would show him what I could do. It was only fair.

"My mom is going to strangle me when I drop out of law school," I said.

He froze. "Is that a yes?"

"Yes," I said. "But I need to tell you something about me."

"What? You can tell me anything."

"Not now, later," I said.

We entwined our fingers and continued up the trail. "By the way, what was Plan B?" I asked.

"Oh. I was going to breach all my contracts and come live with you in San Antonio until you were done with law school. I figured I could settle most of the lawsuits."

"Plan A is definitely better for both of us," I said. "What was Plan C?"

"Plan C was plane tickets for every single weekend to wherever I was. I'd rather have long distance than nothing at all."

We stepped into the clearing where the law school party was definitely on. Barbeque pits and picnic tables with checkered tablecloths were set up along the edge of a crest overlooking the river. The banks were lined with small wooden cabins on stilts. In the large clearing behind the cabins, several families were setting up tents.

"Nice," Gavyn said.

Bree was standing near the edge of the ridge. She was holding a beer in one hand and waving us over with the other.

"Hey!" she said when we were in shouting distance. "Come check this out."

We weaved our way through the small but growing crowd until we reached the edge. "Isn't it pretty?" She gestured over the small cliff.

We were about thirty feet or so above the river, a lazy current of blue and brown. Big, red jagged rocks lined the edge of the cliff. Some people were wading in the shallows below. Others floated by on inner tubes, beers in hand.

"How do you get down there?" Gavyn asked. "This looks like a death pit."

Bree pointed to her right. "Wooden stairs over there, and over here,"—she gestured to her left—"the cliff rock thing gives way to a dirt incline. It's a lot easier to get down over there."

"Cool." I stepped back from the edge, and pulled Bree and Gavyn several yards back with me. Bree was making me nervous. Combining alcohol and heights was never a good idea.

In the few short minutes we had spent on the cliff, more cars were parked in the packed dirt, several more tents had appeared, and the crowd had swelled to at least one hundred people.

I felt a tap against my hip. I looked down into the large brown eyes of a little girl. I guessed she was three or four. She was wearing jean shorts and a red shiny light jacket with a hood. She was holding out a wildflower in her chubby little hand. I took the flower and smiled, crouching down next to her. "Thank you very much."

She gave me a big toothy smile.

"Sorry!" her mom called from a lawn chair nearby. I recognized her from my torts class: Haley. "She's very friendly." She raised her voice. "Vanessa, come back over here. Leave those nice people alone."

The little girl moved closer to the cliff. Her vigilant mom got on her feet and walked toward her. "Vanessa, too close. Stay with Mommy."

It must have happened in a matter of seconds, but it unraveled before me in slow motion. The muddy ground beneath the girl's feet crumbled. The girl slid rapidly to the precipice. Her mom let out the most inhuman, bloodcurdling scream I had ever heard.

Without a thought in my mind, I sprinted to the edge and dove, sliding toward her. I desperately reached for her red jacket as she slid faster on the slippery ground. We both tumbled over the edge.

Chapter 8

I caught her by the hood of her red jacket before we hit the churning water. I pulled her up to my hip and cradled her tightly against my body. She was crying, her eyes squeezed shut.

And just like that, my life was pretty much over.

"It's okay. You're safe." I patted her back as I held her aloft. I was amazed and horrified at what had just happened. I had never tested the boundaries of it before so I had no idea I could move so fast in the air or hold anyone up. I couldn't even feel her weight as we floated.

I looked up. We were below a sharp, narrow outcropping, blocking us from view from the clearing we had fallen from. The waders and swimmers in the water were staring up at me in silence. Beers were forgotten, inner tubes abandoned and floating down the river.

Vanessa's brown eyes popped open. Her little head jerked around as she took in the scenery. Her expressive eyebrows furrowed in concentration when she realized we were not on solid ground.

Like all young children do, she immediately accepted the reality presented to her. "You're an angel," she said.

I smiled back at her, but my own tears betrayed me.

Her mom's frantic cries interrupted my reverie. She was screaming at the top of her lungs. I couldn't make out any words, but I could hear the anguish in her voice. I heard the low tenor of a hysterical male voice. I couldn't tell if it was Gavyn or the girl's father.

I floated up around the outcropping slowly, not wanting to push the boundaries of it while I had precious cargo in my arms.

The mother was lying on the ground, screaming inexplicably. Gavyn and Bree must have sprinted to the stairs leading down to the river, but now they were paused at the top steps, staring at me.

The mother's sobbing cut off in her throat as soon as she saw me. Gavyn met my eyes as I flew over the cliff. He stood and staggered a few steps back, clapping both of his hands over his mouth. Bree grabbed his arm to keep him from falling backwards down the stairs.

Hundreds of other pairs of eyes were watching me. Somebody screamed, but then fell quiet. My fellow classmates were frozen in place, still and silent as statues.

I landed a safe distance away from the edge of the cliff. I tore my eyes away from Gavyn as I bent down to place the girl on the ground.

I turned my attention to Gavyn. He was shaking his head, like he had a fly buzzing around him. My heart collapsed. It was over. He saw what I was and he was afraid.

Haley embraced me. "Thank you. You're an angel. Thank you for saving my little girl." She continued to babble, but I couldn't make out the rest.

I pulled away gently. I needed to go. Now. My mom had told me what I needed to do if I ever got exposed.

Run.

I took one last look at Gavyn, drinking in every detail of his face. "I'm sorry," I whispered.

I turned on my heel and ran down the trail. I thought about flying now I knew I could do it fast, but the last thing I needed was to run into a group of hikers and have more witnesses. Thanks to the long hours in the gym, I was physically prepared to escape.

My logical self took over and started churning out my options. I could make it back to the cabin in six or seven minutes if I pushed myself really hard. All I needed was my wallet. Anything else I had time to grab was extra. Then I would take Gavyn's rental car to the airport. I would get a flight to anywhere I possibly could. My eventual destination was Kansas. My mom would know what to do. She was unlisted and had different last name than me. Surely no one would find me. I would just lay low for a while and then…

Gavyn's voice pierced through my planning. "Stop!" He was running after me. I pushed back the intense longing to stop and speak to him, just touch him one last time.

"Aurora, please!" he yelled again. I risked another peek behind me. His long legs were churning, gaining momentum. He was going to catch up to me.

He grabbed the edge of my shirt, which threw me off balance. We collided and fell, sliding down the trail before running into a tree. I was on my feet in an instant, ready to bolt again. He grabbed my sleeve. "Wait. We need to talk."

I yanked it away, fighting the urge to run into his arms.

"What happened? Is that what you've been hiding from me? What was that?" The words bubbled out of his mouth. "I thought you were gone. Oh, my God, I thought you were dead, and then you just, just, floated back!" His voice was teetering on the edge of hysteria. He collapsed forward, and put his hands on his knees to steady himself.

He straightened and took another step toward me. "Wait, please."

I looked into his perfect eyes one last time. "It's dangerous for me to be here now. I have to go. Please don't tell anyone what you saw. I'm sorry." I took a deep breath, not willing to do what I needed to do. "I love you."

He reached for me. I turned around and tried to push his face out of my mind.

Then, I flew away.

Chapter 9

I flew just below the tree line, not wanting to make any more public appearances today. I moved much faster up here than on the bumpy trail below. I kept my ears alert, ready to land the second I heard a human voice.

Pain ripped through my chest. Losing Gavyn was much worse than I could have imagined. Especially losing him like this.

Tears clouded my vision, but I wiped them away. I could cry later. I needed all my attention focused on my objective. I needed to get out of here and go into hiding, fast.

I made it back to the cabin in three minutes. I grabbed my wallet, keys, and cell phone and threw them in to the partially unpacked bag I had left on the rumpled bedcovers.

Guilt added on to my general misery as Gavyn's rental car roared to life. It was bad enough what I had put him through today without having to deal with a missing car.

I sped down the winding road to the main roads. I finally made it to the interstate. I pushed the car up to eighty-five. I really let the tears come then.

I made it to the airport in twenty minutes. I rushed to the counter of the first airline I saw. The next flight was leaving in thirty-five minutes, and was going to Colorado. I booked it and charged the ridiculous $1600.00 fee on my credit card. I buzzed through security pretty fast. By the time I got to the gate, first class was already boarding. I only had a few minutes to make a not-so-fun call.

"Mom? I'm on my way to Colorado, can you get me a flight to Wichita?"

"What? What's wrong?"

I looked around to make sure nobody was close by. "I flew. In public, and I didn't mean to do it, but I did." I put my hand over my mouth to stop the sobs.

"Okay, baby. Let's calm down. Count to ten with me. One, two, three..."

"Four, five, six," I said in a shaky voice.

"Keep going."

"Seven, eight, nine, ten." By the time I got to ten, my voice had firmed up a bit.

"Good." Her voice was smooth. "I'm going to ask you some questions."

"Okay," I said. "Hurry." She paused as the attendant announced on loudspeaker the boarding of the first fourteen rows.

"How many people saw?" she asked.

"Hundreds, mostly law students."

"Like 100 or 200 or what?" she said.

"Maybe 150."

"Okay. Were there any camera flashes or video recordings?"

I thought back to the moment. I wasn't paying attention, but I didn't remember seeing any, and I told her so.

"Good," she said. "What happened?"

"I saved a little girl who fell off a cliff."

She exhaled loud and slow into the phone. "Okay, let's get you safe. Hang up the phone and text me your flight number. I'll purchase you a flight home, and text you the details. I'll have them leave your ticket at the gate. Okay?"

"Okay," I said.

"Aurora?" she said.

"Yes?"

"I love you. Be careful and stay calm. I'll take care of it from here."

I texted her the flight number and found my seat. I stared at my little phone. It vibrated over and over with calls from Bree and Gavyn. I didn't answer. I finally shut it off and put it in the bottom of my purse when the flight attendant gave me the death stare.

The flight wasn't very long, but it felt like it would never end. I could feel every mile between me and Gavyn. I doubted I would ever come back. My chest hurt, each beat sending webs of pain through my body.

I wanted to be unconscious with a dead, cold sleep where I didn't feel anything.

Instead, I slumped over my chair and studied the tops of my shoes. I was in a precarious situation. Would people come after me? Would I be on the news? Would the government try to take me to study me? Okay, maybe that was a little out there, but who knows?

FLEE

The flight from Colorado to Kansas was worse. By the time I taxied into Wichita, I had some time to process the events of the day, but I was isolated in the airplane so I had no idea what was going on outside the pressurized cabin.

My mom was waiting outside the terminal, leaning against her car. She smiled and pulled me into a hug, but there was tightness around her eyes and the engine was running.

"You don't have any luggage, right?" she said.

"No."

"Get in the car. We'll swing by the house, but then we need to go."

I got in without another word. She climbed in next to me, took off the parking brake, and peeled out of the airport parking lot.

"What is it?" I asked in a small voice.

"It's already on the internet. The San Antonio newspaper has it on their website." She tossed me her smart phone.

She had a San Antonio newspaper website pulled up. Under the headline, "Breaking news: Bizarre story coming out of San Marcos," was a quick blurb: "We've received several eyewitness reports that a three year old child, who fell off a bluff into the Guadalupe river, was rescued by a 'flying' woman. The event happened at a law school gathering, where hundreds of students are claiming they saw a woman fly. In another strange twist, unconfirmed accounts also claim Gavyn Dhaval, a well-regarded British actor, was present at the party. Police are investigating the incident."

I handed it back to her. "Now what?"

"Now we have to hope it doesn't get picked up nationally. But, the fact Gavyn's name is attached to it pretty much guarantees it will." She

89

gave me a pointed look. "I need you to prepare yourself. It could get rough."

We made it to our house in twenty minutes. The small white house with green trim and weirdly long driveway was familiar and safe.

She pulled far up into her driveway, but didn't park in her small, detached garage like she usually did.

My sister, Erica, was waiting inside. She pulled me into a rough hug. "You stupid cow, I miss you!" she said into my ear. When she stepped away, she threw her glance from me to our mother. Erica's eyes were wet, brown hair disheveled, and she looked tired.

My mom gestured her head towards the dark T.V. "Why is that off?"

Erica shook her head. "It hit CNN – I just saw it on the ticker. You've got two messages on your phone from news stations. You guys need to go."

"Go?" I repeated.

"Here." Erica dragged a suitcase off the couch and leaned it against my leg. "I went through all my clothes and packed you some stuff that's too big for me. I think it'll fit. I put a toothbrush in there too."

She unzipped the small front pocket. She placed a chunky old fashioned cell phone in my hand. "This is a pay as you go cell phone. I bought two, and I have the other one. I programmed my number in it. I think it's best we communicate this way."

"Good thinking," Mom said. "My suitcase is in the trunk. We should go."

"Okay." Erica hugged her. "I can't stay at the house because it'll throw the boys out of their school routine, but I'll check in on the house every couple of days."

"Thanks, sweetie. We'll be okay." My mom turned to me. "You ready?"

"Wait." I took a few steps back. "What are we doing?"

My mother answered. "We need to go into hiding."

"Where are we going? Don't you need to work?"

She slung her purse over her shoulder. "I took emergency leave, and I have access to a cabin in the Ozarks. It's empty for the next few months."

"I should probably text Bree and let her know I'm okay." I dug through my purse until I found my cell phone. "I have thirty-three missed calls from Gavyn." The tears pricked behind my eyes again.

"You can't call him, or Bree, or anyone else. Throw away your cell phone, forget law school, and forget the boy. This is life or death."

She snatched her keys off the table and went outside. I followed her on weak, shaky legs. Tears spilled out my eyes and made the world blurry and strange.

I curled myself up in a ball in the passenger seat. She said little, other than to force me to drink a bottle of water every now and again.

A few hours passed where my mom gripped the steering wheel a little too hard and checked her rearview mirror constantly. Finally, she stopped at an isolated gas station in the middle of nowhere. I was staring at my cell phone in my hands. I had so many missed calls and texts it was displaying an error message that my memory was full.

She put her hand on my leg. "I'm sorry this has happened, but you can't call them back. I can't let you put yourself in any danger." She patted my knee. "Make a clean break. Get rid of it."

She shot me a look that was a mixture of resolve and pity before she stepped out of the car to refill the gas tank. I got out too and threw my little bright blue phone in the trash. It was my last connection to Gavyn, and it started a fresh round of tears.

We made the eight hour drive in one night, arriving at the lake cabin in the wee hours of the morning. It was a small two-bedroom on the shore of a beautiful lake. A small dock jutted out the back into the moonlit water. On any other occasion, I would have been thrilled with the location.

It was fully furnished, with two couches and a flat screen television, an open kitchen, and bedrooms on either side of the living room, both furnished with queen size beds. The décor was dated, but it was neat and well kept.

I sat on the back porch for three hours, leaning against the railing, sipping a glass of water.

I watched the sun rise for the first time in a long time. Boats flitted across the surface of the lake in the distance. Birds circled and swooped in a magnificent rush to catch their watery prey.

She came outside when the morning changed from dawn to light. She sat beside me on the porch, scooted closer, and slung an arm over my shoulder. "You okay?"

"I don't know."

"You need to eat, or go to bed. Preferably both. You can't sit out here forever," she said.

"I'll sleep then." I squeezed her hand before I went inside.

After twenty-four straight hours of being awake, merciful sleep rendered me unconscious in short order.

Chapter 10

I dreamt of Gavyn.

I dreamed we were back in San Antonio. He gave me a bracelet and told me he loved me. I was floating away from him. I tried to sink back down to him, but I just kept floating away, higher and higher until I could no longer see him.

I woke up covered in sweat. I shot up to a seated position as the events of the previous day and night rolled into my head. There was a soft murmur of voices from a T.V. set, the smell of coffee, and a clank of dishes.

I showered and finally changed out of my now stinky clothes. I dug through the suitcase packed with my sister's clothes. Luckily, we were about the same size. I found a pair of running shorts and a soft cotton t-shirt to wear.

Mom stood from the couch as I came in. "Morning." She wrapped me in her arms and gave me a super-long mom hug. She put one hand on my shoulder and used the other one to tip my chin up so she could see my face. "You okay, kiddo? How are you feeling?"

"Yes, I think so." I pulled out of her reach so I could look around. "What time is it?"

"3:00 in the afternoon. I picked up some groceries. I'll make you a sandwich."

"I'm not hungry," I said.

"You're eating anyways," she said.

I sat down on the couch in front of the T.V. while she bustled around in the kitchen. "So, how bad is it?"

"Not good, but not as bad as I thought. It's been picked up on all the major networks. They've tracked down your life, your law school, and me. I don't think the family of the kid has a lot of credibility, especially since Gavyn's rep is refusing to comment. The cops have said they think some drug use was going on. Erica said there are a few news vans camped outside the house."

She sat next to me and put the sandwich and a diet soda on the table in front of me. "Eat, drink." She gestured toward the T.V. "Most of the new stations are painting this as a human interest story. I don't think the claim you can fly is being taken seriously, but my home phone must be ringing off the hook. I had eighty nine voicemails when I called in this morning. I called the phone company and had the number disconnected. I'll wait a few weeks to see if I need to move. If we stay in hiding, I think this may blow over."

"Whoa, whoa." I put down my sandwich. "If anyone needs to move, it's me. When this settles down, you go home."

"We'll talk about this later," she said, "but, over the next couple of days you'll need to call the law school to let them know you will be withdrawing. You can't go back there."

"Fine. I was going to drop out anyways."

Her head snapped up. "What?"

I fingered the bracelet Gavyn had given me. "Gavyn asked me to be with him. I was going to withdraw from law school. I was going to go with him everywhere: L.A., London, on location when he shot movies, press tours, the whole nine yards. I was going to see the world. That's what we had planned. Now, it's all gone." This time I didn't bother trying to hold back the tears. I dissolved into a mess of sobs. My paper plate flipped over and spilled my sandwich onto the floor, but I didn't care. I cried, and it was loud and it felt kind of good.

She pulled me across the couch so I was lying on her lap. "Let it out. It's okay." She stroked my hair and cheek. "I'm sorry, honey. I didn't realize you'd gotten so serious."

I cried until I was all dried up. It was dark when we stood to go outside and watch the sun set. We sat on the end of the dock, drinking cool beer and slicing the surface of the smooth water with our feet.

"I'm sorry," she said. "It's not fair to you. I know. You have no idea how he feels about your ability?"

"The look in his eyes when he saw me was…" I swallowed the icky bump in my throat. "It was pretty clear he was afraid."

"But he chased you. Why would he chase you if was afraid?"

"It doesn't matter. I didn't have time to stick around and chat." I paused to take another swig of beer. "This can't be good for him either, all this press."

We finished our beers, ate dinner, and then crashed. I hadn't physically exerted myself all day, but I felt a deep, dead tired in my mind and body. I had a dreamless night.

I woke up the next morning to the insistent purr of boats buzzing across the lake. I resisted the urge stay in bed and mope. I needed to wake up and function, or at least pretend to function.

My mom was standing in front of the living room television with a mug in her hand. She was as still as ice.

I focused my attention on the television. It was a sensationalist national news network. It showed people camped outside my mom's home carrying signs and chanting I was the devil. They were from some weird backwoods church. The photographers duly interviewed these people. Their deep wrinkled, gap toothed faces spoke into the camera.

"She doesn't go to church, but she can fly. She is not of the angels, she is of the devil!" a hateful woman shouted at the camera. "We must rid the world of her evil. She must come forward and accept her punishment!"

"What a bunch of idiots! Why the hell is this on the national news?" I said.

"No one takes them seriously. I don't understand why they are covering this either. This is what I'm afraid of though. Those crazy hillbillies probably have guns and if we were there, they might try to hurt you. Not that they would get very far."

The newscaster returned to the story about me and reported several death threats for me had been called into local news stations in Wichita. That one caused the color to drain out of my mother's face.

I accepted the news calmly. I had lived in fear of being exposed for the past ten years. Now all I would have to do is face the consequences.

"I think it's time you learn to shoot a gun," she said. "I can protect you now, but you need to be able to take care of yourself in the future." She snapped up the remote and turned off the T.V. "Enough garbage.

Get dressed. Let's check out the hiking trail around the lake." Her mouth was set in a firm line. She had bright red spots on her cheeks. I felt sorry for anyone who messed with her today.

We spent the rest of the day exploring the lake, avoiding people, and trying to keep our minds off the brewing media storm.

When I went to bed later on that night, I stared at the ceiling for hours. I didn't feel anything at all; no fear, no pain, nothing. It was abnormal, but better than pain.

The news stations were still talking about me the next day.

The hateful protestors were still there, albeit in much smaller numbers. A much larger group of people had shown up, fighting against the actions of the hateful. They were camping out, keeping the crazies off of my mom's property, and telling them to leave. They interviewed one of the new group members.

"This is ridiculous. She probably can't fly, and even if she can, who cares? This family has lived here for ten years. They're good people. We won't let these hate mongers run them out of town. She saved a life. Why are people making such a big deal out of this?"

I was relieved someone was standing up for me and my mom when we couldn't do it ourselves. It restored my faith in humanity. Well, somewhat restored my faith in humanity.

"Thank God," my mom said. "I was starting to think the whole world was completely mad. Maybe this will die down." She took a long drink of her third cup of coffee and set it down on the table. "Let's go canoeing," she suggested brightly.

"Sure, Mom." And we did. We stayed away from the T.V. and phone.

We returned to the cabin several hours later. She cooked some steaks on the compact charcoal grill outside. We ate in front of the television. I mentally braced myself for any more Aurora related coverage.

A pretty brunette appeared on the screen of a national news network. "And now returning to the story grabbing national headlines. Spectators claimed a woman, Aurora Lockette, saved their child by flying to catch her when the cliff the child was standing on gave way. Additional reports surfaced Lockette was with Gavyn Dhaval at the time, a notable Hollywood figure. It seems that at least this part of the bizarre story is true. Today, for the very first time since these events unfolded, Gavyn Dhaval released a written statement as follows:

'I'd like to clear up some misconceptions about events that recently transpired. Earlier this week, I was with Aurora Lockette. She was brave and alert enough to lunge after a little girl who was falling off a cliff, saving her life. Aurora caught the girl before she went over the edge and pulled her back up. I can only imagine the trauma this family experienced at almost watching their child die. However, I can no longer remain silent while they continue to make ridiculous assertions that Ms. Lockette flew. These are absurd and hurtful, as they have caused unwanted attention and hate to be directed to Ms. Lockette. I would ask the media respect Ms. Lockette's privacy. It is unfortunate a heroic but very human act has been turned into a hate-filled media circus.' "

"Wow," my mom said.

I'm sure his agent and rep were cringing he would have to publicly comment on such a ridiculous situation. Pain broke through my numbness and threatened to crash over me.

I excused myself and hid behind the closed doors of my bedroom. In the darkness, I thought about everything I had lost.

I slept in late the next morning. When I woke up, my mom was stretched out on the couch in the living room. "Morning," she said as I trotted in with a cup of coffee. "I think we can go back in a couple of days. The news broke this morning the family retracted their statements and apologized. They 'admitted' they were looking for some publicity. All your classmates are still refusing interviews. That was early this morning and there hasn't been a single story again," she said. "I don't know what prompted them to do this, but I'm sure glad they did. This family and Gavyn are covering for you now. Maybe it'll be enough to get everyone else to back off too."

Sure enough, four days later we were loading up the car to return to Kansas. Erica reported there were no visitors to my mom's home in several days. The story completely dropped out of the media. My mom had her phone service restored under a new number. There wasn't a single errant message.

I had time to think about what the future might hold for me as we drove back. I had withdrawn from law school, knowing my situation would be ingrained on my classmates' minds forever.

When we pulled into the driveway, I hadn't come up with a plan and I was exhausted. I went straight to my old bedroom. My sister's boyfriend had kindly driven to San Antonio and vacated my apartment. Boxes of my stuff were stacked in neat rows, filling half of the room. My furniture was in storage in my sister's basement. I was grateful to have most of my stuff back. I still had a stash in the cabin I'd shared with Gavyn, but that was gone forever.

"Aurora!" My mom's voice floated through my half open door. "You have a piece of mail." I walked into the dining room, where she had left the large ivory envelope with a red flap on the table. My name and my mom's address were written in calligraphy. I picked it up and flipped over the envelope a couple times, feeling the heavy weight of the fancy paper. There was no return address. It was postmarked from Fairbanks, Alaska.

"Quit playing with it and open it," she called from the kitchen.

And so I did. I read the note twice, struggling to understand the words neatly handwritten on the plain ivory paper inside.

Aurora,

We have been watching your family bloodline for several generations. Somehow we missed you. For that, I am sorry. We were able to gain control over the situation with the media this time. However, you are still in grave danger.

There are others like you. You are not alone.

We will be making contact with you shortly.

Chapter 11

I must have dropped the letter, because it was gracefully spiraling toward the floor.

My mom paused her sweeping. "Are you okay? Is it something bad?"

I didn't answer. Was it a joke? An unknown relative?

She stooped down to pick it up, reading as she stood. "Is this real?" She tossed the letter on the table, strode over to the door and locked the deadbolt. She methodically went through every window in the house, checking to make sure they were latched. I heard the click of her gun safe from the bedroom.

"Mom! Just chill. It's not a threatening letter. And it was sent from Alaska, not here."

"I know, but it's a little strange, and it's been an eventful week. I'm just taking some precautions." She came back into the dining room. We both sat on the table with the letter between us. We stared at it, as if it would reveal its secrets.

Finally, she spoke. "Okay, there are two basic options as I see it. Let's start with the simplest explanation first. It's a joke. Someone who saw the news stories is trying to mess with you. That's the most likely scenario."

I shook my head in disagreement. "From Alaska? Someone in freaking Alaska saw the news last week, composed this creepy little letter, found out your home address, and dropped it in the mail four days ago, exactly when the media storm died down?"

She leaned back in her chair and crossed her arms. "You're right. This letter was mailed the same time Gavyn and the family released their statements. The media interest evaporated. I didn't realize the timeline coincided. But it still could just be a coincidence."

"What's your second scenario?" I said.

"It's legit. I've always wondered if there are more people like you out there. The letter mentioned bloodline, and your great grandmother was institutionalized for delusions. Maybe she said she could fly." She picked up the letter again. "I wonder if there would be some sort of support group or something. I guess that could make sense."

"I'm not an alcoholic. I don't need a support group. Do you really think there's an anonymous secret support group for the gravity challenged in Fairbanks, Alaska?"

"Well, when you say it like that, I guess it does sound surreal." Her face became more serious. "Let's face it though, your life is pretty surreal. Stranger things have happened."

I took the letter back and read the words one more time. "The mysterious author said they will make contact with me soon. Let's just keep our guard up, and see what happens. If no one contacts me, then we know it's a joke. If someone contacts me, we'll go from there." I smiled at her. "Try not to shoot anyone, okay?"

"Fine. I'll try to restrain myself. For now." I couldn't tell if she was joking or not.

I was awake in bed for several hours watching the occasional light flash across the ceiling from passing cars. I thought about the possibilities hinted at in the letter, providing a welcome retreat from my heartache. Could there really be a group of people out there like me? If it was genetic, why did my mom and sister remain firmly planted on earth's surface at all times?

I tried not to get too excited about the letter, but I couldn't help it. Nothing about the letter made sense, but logic rarely prevailed in my world.

As usual, the pain over losing Gavyn was still working at the corner of my mind. Alone, in the dark, I let it wash over me. I cried into my pillow, soaking it with my tears. I could only hope as time went on, the pain would at least dull to a more manageable level.

It didn't. Boredom defined my life in Wichita. I didn't go to school, I didn't have a job. The novelty of having nothing to do quickly wore off.

My one salvation was exercise. I could run eight miles at a time and spend hours in the gym lifting weights.

I was fit, but I was clueless. I couldn't figure out if I wanted to go back to school. If I did, I wasn't sure if I would finish law school or do something else. My job options were somewhat limited in Wichita. A liberal arts degree was almost completely useless on that front.

I allowed a few days to slip by until I woke up determined to spend my day productively. The least I could do was help out my mom while I was living like a useless bum in her house. I left for the grocery store, taking my old economy car my sister's boyfriend had retrieved from San Antonio. I took the time to peruse the aisles and compare prices. It felt good to be doing something constructive with my time.

I was walking out of the store when a short, wiry forty-something man with bright blond hair approached me. Thick sunglasses hid his eyes, but he still looked vaguely familiar. I stiffened and wrapped my hand around the pepper spray, for once glad my mom insisted I carry it with me wherever I go.

"You received our letter?" He had a faint eastern European accent.

"What? Is this a joke?"

He glanced behind him before he spoke. "It's not a joke. Please believe me. We cannot talk any further here." He handed me an envelope. "It's time we met. Here is an address of a small café just outside city limits. Meet me tomorrow at two in the afternoon. Bring your mother if it will make you feel more comfortable. It's a public place, but we should be able to speak privately. I'll have some answers for you. Please come." He started to walk away, and then paused. "There are others."

He disappeared into the crowd of people walking into the grocery store. I was transfixed, gripping the handles of the shopping cart until my knuckles turned white. Eventually, I managed to get a hold of myself and go back to my car.

Once home, I booted up the computer and looked up the address of the diner. It was a small place, just like he said. I would go. I would tell my mom about it, but I would definitely go.

She wasn't nearly as excited about it as I was.

"This whole thing is really bizarre," she said. "I don't know about this." She was sitting at the table, pinching the top of her nose with her eyes closed, something she only did when she was really upset.

"It's in a diner, a public place. I'm going. If you would like to come, you are more than welcome," I said.

"Fine. I will be armed," she said.

I was practically bouncing in the passenger seat when we pulled into the diner parking lot the next day. My mom wore a baggy t-shirt to conceal the gun she was wearing on her person. She looked at me, resting her arms over the steering wheel. "Are you sure about this?"

I appraised the small, old metallic diner. There were a couple of trucks and one shiny black car parked outside. "Yes."

A girl my age behind the counter took orders from the bar and waited on the tables. It was simple fare: hamburgers, hotdogs and waffles.

The man was there, waiting in a booth at the far end of the restaurant. He sat with his hands folded in front of him. He was pale, and leanly muscled, with grey eyes like me, except his were a steely light grey, almost blue.

Without sunglasses, I recognized him. I'd seen him before back in San Antonio, at the grocery store and the bookstore.

He smiled as I settled in across from him. "I'm so glad you decided to come. My name is Konstantin." He reached across the table and shook my hand. He directed his gaze to my mom. "You must be Aubrey. Thank you for being here."

"Are you alone?" she asked.

"Yes, I am the only one here."

The waitress took our order. When she left, Konstantin clasped his hands together. "I know this must be very strange for you. I understand in order for us to communicate further, I must first earn your trust, and your mother's." He gestured toward my mom. "The best way I can earn you trust is to give you some information about yourself, and your ability. I must warn you, some of this will be surprising. Please remember we are in a public place."

He turned his head, scanning the restaurant with his eyes. When he was done, he lowered his voice. "It starts off as almost, shall we say...levitation, and for some, that's as far as it gets. For others, it can be much, much more. It's something you have to control at all times, which clearly you have been able to teach yourself how to do. At times when you are very sleepy or in an extreme emotional state, be it good or bad, it is harder to control. Sound familiar?"

He must have received some affirmation from the expression on my face, because he continued.

"Your ability, I suspect, is one of the strongest we have ever heard of, if the account of your feat is true."

He paused while the waitress put down a burger for me and coffees for him and my mom, then left.

"There are others. Many, many others. All over the world." He tore open a sugar packet and emptied it into his coffee. "We've been able to trace some, but not all, back to specific bloodlines. The bloodlines are from every race and ethnicity you can imagine." He paused. "Please, eat your food. I'll explain while you eat."

I numbly took a bite, forcing myself to chew so he would keep talking.

"Those of us with abilities try and find each other. We have been watching you and trying to protect you since you've been exposed. It appears our efforts with the media were successful." He smiled. "I'm assuming you will both have questions. Please, ask me anything."

"You've been following me," I blurted out through a mouthful of burger.

"We protected you in San Antonio. Yes."

"What?" My mom looked pissed.

"Why?" I breathed.

"Because they were getting too close," he said.

"They?"

"There are dangers for us, but don't worry. We won't let anything get through."

For the first time since my exposure, a cold hard, fear blossomed in my chest. "Who? Who would hurt me?"

"Not who, what." His voice dropped so low we both leaned forward to hear him. "The dark ones. We call them Shyama. This is something I cannot explain in full right now. Not here."

Whoa. The universe became fuzzy around the edges of my vision. My mom put her hand on my arm. "Deep breaths, baby." She left her cool hand on my arm, but refocused her gaze on Konstantin. "How can we know if you are telling the truth about all this?"

"I'm one of the others. I can show you my abilities. I have no reason to lie."

"Where are the others?" I whispered.

"All over the place. Some choose to isolate themselves and live together, in small towns and villages they create themselves. Others choose to mix in with normal society."

"You're telling me there is a secret society of flyers?" I said.

"No. A secret society of those with special abilities. There are many kinds."

My mom slammed her fist down on the table, making both me and Konstantin jump. "Enough! How do we even know if any of this crap is true?"

Konstantin smiled. "It's time Aurora met the others. There, she can learn everything."

"I'd like to meet some people like me."

"No. This is too dangerous," my mom said. "We don't even know who you are, or what you are."

"I understand your fear. I have someone here in town with me. If you are willing to meet in private, we will show you our abilities, so you know you are like us." He slipped an envelope across the table. "There is much, much more to discuss. I do no want to lead anything to you so we must take precautions. Please meet me in this hotel room tonight at 8:00. The address and key are inside." His eyes slid to my mom. "As I have said before, we will never harm you, but I understand if you continue to choose to arm yourself."

He took my hand. I stiffened, but let him. "You are very precious to us. You have much to learn about yourself, and very little time to learn it. Please come tonight."

He threw a fifty dollar bill on the table and left without another word.

My mom watched him leave. She moved so she was sitting across from me. "I don't know about all of this. How do we know if these are the good guys?"

"Something tells me they're not bad. Why would someone go through all this trouble to contact me if they just wanted to hurt me?" I pushed the plate with my half eaten burger away from me. "What else am I going to do? Sit here? Apply for jobs day in and day out?"

When we got back to the house, I sat on the front porch and waited for the dark to come. My brain flitted over all the things Konstantin had said. I rolled the ideas over and over in my head, trying to imagine if they were real. It didn't seem possible, but then again what I could do was not possible either.

After the night fully settled in, I washed my face, changed my clothes, and got in the car with my mom. "Are you sure you're okay?" she asked as we drove toward the hotel.

"Yeah," I said. "It's sinking in, I think."

"I'm glad it's sinking in for you."

We pulled up to the chain hotel shortly before eight. She paused outside the door to the appointed room. "Hold on." She placed her hand inside her purse strapped across her shoulder.

"What are you doing?"

"I can shoot through the purse. No need to even pull it out," she said. "Let's go in."

"Right on, soldier."

Konstantin answered at the first knock. He stepped out and threw a glance in each direction before letting us in.

"Were you followed?" He directed his question to my armed mother. "No."

Inside the room, the dark shades were drawn closed, but all the lamps were on, casting the furnishings in a bright light. A redheaded woman, about the same age of Konstantin, stood near by.

"Aurora, Aubrey, this is Carmen. She's my wife."

Carmen stepped forward to shake my hand. She was petite and wiry, like Konstantin. She had shocking aqua eyes and a light smattering of freckles across her nose and cheeks. She released my hand quickly, but her expression was warm. "Aurora, it's so nice to meet you. I'm so glad you came."

She turned to my mom. "I understand your caution. I will not be offended if you prefer to keep your hand on your firearm."

She withdrew her hand and shook Carmen's. "I don't need to have my hand on it to use it quickly. I'm glad you understand I have to protect my daughter."

Konstantin cleared his throat. "I'll cut to the chase. I'm here to show you our abilities, so you know you can trust us, so you know we are the same. These are deep secrets we carefully guard. I ask you protect them." He stared at my mom as he spoke.

Without another word, he drifted gracefully to the ceiling.

"You are like me!" I dropped my purse on the floor and let it happen. Soon, I ascended so I was eye level with Konstantin.

"At some point we will need to spend some time together so I can assess the extent of your abilities. You have excellent control," he said.

We both looked down. My mom was sitting on the floor, her mouth open.

"Why don't you two come down?" Carmen said, gesturing toward my shocked mother.

I sank to the ground. "Mom, are you okay?"

"Yes. I...I just never thought I would..." Her voice trailed off again. "It was little shocking to see two people flying, okay?" She pointed at Carmen. "Can you fly too?

"No. May I take your hand, Aurora? It's not necessary, but it does help me."

"Sure."

She took my hand, holding it in hers for a few seconds before she spoke. "You are feeling very happy right now, but you are riddled with pain. Your heart is broken. You can see his face in your dreams. It's haunting you." She paused. "You feel your ability is unfair, because you can't have the one thing you want. Would you like me to continue?"

"I guess."

She looked at my wrist. "Your bracelet. It was made for you. You haven't told your mother, but it's from him."

I pulled my hand back. "You could have just said you were a telepath."

"I'm not a mind reader. I'm very sensitive. I can sense emotions, see bonds between people," she said. "I have a strong sense of premonition. I can identify danger if it is nearby. I can sense if someone seeks to harm me or the ones around me. I can see if someone intends to do well."

"Oh." I guessed her gift was much more powerful than she was letting on. My poor mom had gone from shocked to pale and tired-looking.

"Mom?"

"I'm fine. I'm just a little overwhelmed."

Carmen whispered something in Konstantin's ear. Konstantin led us to the door. "You must go. You've been here too long. It would be bad to lead them to Aurora, but worse to lead them to you, Aubrey. We will leave this area as well."

My mom snapped back into her old self. "Good. We need some time to think." She shook hands with Konstantin and Carmen. "Thank you both for being so open. Your secrets are safe with me."

Carmen answered. "Your words are true."

My mom shot her a wary look as she pulled me out the door.

When we got home, she brewed two cups of tea. "You want to talk?"

"No. I want to crawl into a little cave and sleep until this is all over."

She sat next to me on the couch. "We both have a lot to process. Sometimes when you go to bed with a problem, you wake up with a solution."

I was almost glad Gavyn was out of the picture. Almost. At least he would be safe. I only cried for a few minutes that night before sinking into a deep sleep.

Chapter 12

The next morning, I woke up to lukewarm coffee in the pot and an empty house. I braced myself for another day, wondering what new information could possibly be revealed. Before I could begin to process the events of the past couple days, I needed caffeine. Lots of it.

I drank reheated coffee and watched the national news. The world was still full of huge problems, much bigger than me. The damn phone rang before I was even halfway done with my cup.

"Aurora, it's Konstantin."

"Er, yes?"

"I'm sorry to do this, but you need to start packing. I'll pick you up in fifteen minutes." His accent was stronger than I remembered.

"What are you talking about? Packing for what?" I said.

"As much as you can in the next few minutes. Actually, it's not important what you pack. Get your passport and be ready to go."

"Are you on crack? Where am I going?"

"I attracted their attention. They're getting close. If you stay any longer, they will find you, your mom, and your sister. We can't protect them all."

The familiar panic darted around my mind. "The Shyama?"

"Yes. We don't have time. Get ready. We can call Aubrey on the way out. I've called in some people to keep an eye on her." He paused. "You have to trust me. If you don't come with me, they will find you, and they will find your family, and they will die. You have fourteen minutes until I get there." The line went dead in my hands.

I stared at the phone in my hand, willing for it to provide me with more information. "Damn it!" I slammed it down.

I threw some clothes into a duffel bag, fumbling with my passport and drivers license with shaking hands. I wrote out a quick, jagged note.

A horn honked outside, and I knew it was for me. I threw the duffel bag over my shoulder and took one last look at home, taking in the green furniture and beaded lamps. I didn't know if I would ever see it again. Tears clouded my vision as I walked outside and climbed into the waiting car.

"It's okay," Carmen said, twisting to look at me from the front seat while Konstantin peeled out and took off at an ungodly speed. "We just need to put some miles in. Your mother and sister will be fine. I promise."

"What's going on?"

"They can track us more easily if we are in a group and one member is unprotected. Since we showed up, and you are unprotected, they moved in. We need to leave so they don't find you. They will use any means necessary to get to you, including your family."

"What? How am I unprotected?" I was crying again, but I didn't try to stop it.

"It will all be clear very soon. You'll be safe in Alaska. We have special protections in place there to hide us from them. When you are hidden, your family will be in no danger."

"Will I see them again? My family?"

Carmen rotated in her seat again so she was facing me. "Yes, once you are protected, you can move around more freely without attracting attention. Don't worry. You will see them again."

"Aren't you protecting me?"

"It's complicated. We can talk more when we are safe. Please try and relax. They are drawn to fear and anguish."

"Right, I just chill out here while dark monsters you won't talk about chase me."

"Call your mom."

I called Erica first.

"Erica, it's me."

"Yeah, I know your voice. What number are you calling from?"

"I have to leave town. I'll be gone for a while. I need you to do something for me."

"What the hell are you talking about? Where are you going?"

"I don't have time to explain. Look after Mom, okay? She's going to freak out in about five minutes. Go pick her up from work, like right now."

"Look here, I don't know what bullshit drama you are trying to pull now, but if you think you can just call me up and—"

"Please, listen to me. I'm serious. Take care of Mom, okay? Promise me?"

"Are you okay? What the fuck is going on—"

I broke the connection and made the second, much more difficult call to my mother.

"I have to leave town with Konstantin and Carmen."

"What? No. Absolutely not. We can talk about this when I get home."

"I'm already gone. The bad ones are coming and I have to leave so they don't find you and Erica. Okay? I'm going to be safe, and you are going to be safe. Don't freak out, and don't come looking for me. Don't report me missing. Carry your gun. I love you. I'm so sorry." I wiped my nose with my sleeve so I wouldn't sniffle on the phone. "I have to hang up now."

"Don't. Let's talk about this. I can protect you—"

"I'm so sorry." I hung up the phone.

Carmen took the phone out of my hand. "She can sense the danger as well. She'll do what you ask."

"Thanks, but fuck off. You don't know her."

The look on her face told me I hurt her. She looked like a sad little bird that just flew into a window. She didn't say anything back, but she sank deeper into her seat and seemed intent on looking out the window.

I leaned against the door, watching the scenery fly by impossibly fast. Tears rolled down my cheeks.

I must have fallen asleep because when I woke up, we were in Colorado. I craned my head to read the green numbers on the console. Only two and a half hours had passed by, but we were already halfway to Denver. I didn't dare ask how fast Konstantin was driving, because it usually took me about seven hours to drive from Wichita to Denver.

Soon we were checking in at the airport counter for a flight bound to Alaska. I slept most of the unbelievably long flight, though the stewardess woke me up a couple of times and instructed me to walk around to avoid blood clots.

I really woke up when we started to make our descent in Fairbanks. Densely forested mountains surrounded flat clearings with cars, buildings, and parking lots. A river snaked through the middle of the city. From the runway, Fairbanks looked like a miniature toy town compared with the congested Denver airport.

We got into a rugged SUV with giant tires in long term parking at the airport. "This is ours. You need an all terrain vehicle out here." Konstantin lifted me so I could climb into the backseat.

He drove through the small city. We passed city limits and continued on the bumpy highway. He turned on several side streets until we were on a narrow, unmarked dirt road. The branches of trees and tall plants brushed against the side and bottom of the SUV as we inched along. I grabbed the bottom of the seat so my head wouldn't slam into the roof of the car.

After several miles of rugged country, a tall iron gate appeared, blocking the road. Scary looking ten feet tall barbed wire fence sat on either side. My eyes traced the path of the fence. It disappeared into a dense tree line.

As soon as we approached, it swung open. "We have great security." He gestured up to the cameras mounted on the gate. "Mostly for show. We really don't need all the modern technology. You'll understand why soon." After another half mile of bumpy dirt road, it smoothed into a cracked but paved road.

Buildings clustered around the road; several small simple wood cabins, some larger wooden houses, and some industrial looking warehouses.

Carmen chimed in. "Like many small villages in Alaska, we are self sustaining for the most part. We have to travel in to town occasionally to get supplies, but we have almost everything here. This is one of the largest member villages in the world. We have about twelve-hundred people here."

They pulled up to one of the larger cabins. "This is our home. You can stay with us. We have extra bedrooms," Carmen said.

I got out of the SUV, taking in the beautiful mountains, crisp air, and the forest around me. It was a pleasant sixty or so degrees. "September will be here before you know it, so enjoy the heat while it lasts," she said, intruding on my thoughts in more ways than one.

I followed them into the cabin. It had one large central room filled with plush couches and a flat screen television. A large fireplace dominated the center of the room. The second floor was open, with pretty exposed wood beams marking the high ceiling. "The guest room is up there," she said, gesturing up the stairs.

It was beautiful, with pale lavender walls and deep black bedspread, and a small, attached bathroom. The window framed the pretty deep evergreen forest just outside. I sank into the small rocking chair in front of the window.

Carmen interrupted my pity party. She placed a cool hand on my face, turning me so I had nowhere else to look but at her. "I'm sorry you are hurting." She closed her eyes for a few seconds. "It worked. They lost the trail. Your family is safe. Why don't you call your mother?

There's a phone on the nightstand." She left the room and I practically lunged for the phone.

"Mom?"

"Where are you? Are you safe?"

"I'm fine. I'm in Alaska, somewhere near Fairbanks."

"Did they take you? Because you can hang up this phone and call 911 before they even know you've made another call."

"I came on my own accord. I believe them. I trust them. For now, at least," I said. "You haven't called the police or anything, have you?"

"No."

"Good, don't. I've got it."

"Tell me where you are. I can be there in a day."

It took me the better part of an hour to talk her out of coming after me. She finally agreed not to do anything rash.

It was early evening, though the bright sun outside gave no indication of the day ending. I joined Carmen in the kitchen.

"Do you like lasagna?"

"Sure," I said. "Can I help you with anything?"

"No, sit down and keep me company. I'm sure you have some questions."

"Where's Konstantin?" I asked.

"He's in one of the buildings you saw on the strip."

"And pray tell, what is the strip? I'm guessing we are not talking Vegas?"

"The strip is what we call the paved road in the middle of town."

"Where are the other settlements like this one?" I asked.

"Everywhere. In North America, they are here, Texas, Pennsylvania, Florida, Washington State, New Mexico, Washington D.C., and

Tennessee. The largest is in New Mexico, up in the mountains. Most people with abilities choose to live on their own, mixing in with normal society. They know about us and how to contact us. They travel to see us occasionally." She pulled some ingredients out of the cabinet. "We're in almost any country you can think of. Some groups are smaller than others."

"Why do you live here?"

"We both work for the organization. Most of the people who live here do."

The smell of the meat she was browning reached my nose, and I was suddenly very hungry.

"How did your conversation with your mom go?" she asked.

"Good. She seems a lot calmer than I thought she would be."

"I'm not too surprised to hear that," Carmen remarked as she put the large lasagna in the oven. "She seems to have a tinge of ability, a sensitive like me. She probably understands on some level all this had to happen." She closed the oven. "You are much calmer, I can tell. Konstantin will be home soon and we can all talk over dinner. We have a lot of ground to cover."

Konstantin returned shortly. He kissed Carmen on the cheek and then invited me to sit down for dinner. We settled into the picnic style table next to the kitchen. Carmen served me the warm, delicious lasagna. Konstantin produced a bottle of wine of which I eagerly drank two glasses. My brain was still struggling to comprehend the events of the past few days.

After I had finally satisfied my voracious appetite, I sat silently in my seat, appraising Konstantin and Carmen across the table. I had just placed my entire life in their hands. I still wasn't sure if it was the right decision.

Konstantin cleared his throat and set his glass down. "The organization has three major goals. First and foremost is protection. We offer protection from them, media exposure, and outside knowledge. Keeping our secret is paramount to our survival, on many different levels. Second, we seek to identify and educate those who have ability. Third, to figure out why we exist. We do a lot of research, including genetic, to figure out where our ability comes from."

"Is there a brochure or something that covers all this?" I poured a third glass of wine against my better judgment, but I needed to be drunk to continue to have this eerily calm conversation. "And? What has your research provided? What's the answer?"

Konstantin smiled. "The prevailing thought has been we are the natural next step in human evolution. But if we are evolving, we should be increasing in number, and we are not. Also, since the ability is not always tied to a specific bloodline, we believe it's not so simple."

"I don't understand."

"We must have a purpose, more than simple genetics or micro-evolution. Some things are beyond the scope of simple nucleotide base pairs."

"Like?"

Carmen and Konstantin exchanged a look. Carmen spoke first. "It's a lot to know on your first night here. Perhaps we can—"

"No. I have a right to know." I used my hand to cover a burp. "And I'm moderately drunk so I can totally handle it."

"She's right. It's our number one priority for her, to protect her. She should know what it entails," he said. He took another long drink of his wine, finishing it, before he continued. "Every person with ability has a handler. This handler is sometimes an ordinary person, but sometimes another person with abilities. Once you have a handler, you will be protected."

"A handler? Are you freaking kidding me?" The word sounded strange to my ears. I gulped the rest of my drink too. "Okay, so I need a handler. Can't you just set it up?"

"It's not that simple. We can't choose one for you. It just kind of happens. When you meet the handler, you bond with them and they become your protector. Once they bond with you as your handler, they will change," Konstantin said.

I put both my hands flat on the table, palms down. "What the hell are you talking about? I don't know what that means."

Konstantin answered. "It's an intangible bond. You can't will to have it with someone. I can't go find it for you. It moves into place when handler is ready. Your handler shares your life span, no matter how long it is. They will age at your exact pace. They will be able to sense danger and prevent exposure. Their presence makes it hard for people to see your ability. Most importantly, when you have a handler, they can't track you."

"How do you know my mom is not my handler?"

Carmen answered. "I can see the handler bond. It's not there. I'm sorry. I wish it was. Plus, when you bond on that level, you just...know."

"Okay, let's review. There is a person out there who will be my handler. I have no control over this, and neither do they. When the time is right, we will bond or whatever, and then I will be protected?"

"Yes," Konstantin answered.

"But I want to go home. I have a family."

"We must wait until the handler finds you. Your handler won't know it either until the bond is created. Most likely, you haven't met them yet. Whoever it is, they're not in your life right now. I'm sorry," Konstantin said.

I stared at the surface of the table, examining the irregular, circular lines in the natural wood. I was too close to losing it to look anywhere else. I was stuck here. I was alone. I didn't know any of these people. I was living in a poorly scripted science fiction B movie.

"How do you know I'm safe here? If I don't have a handler, can't they find me anyways?" I asked.

"We have several gifted people here, including blockers. They block outside interest in us from the locals, for one thing. Most importantly for you, they can block them from tracking us. They make this place a fortress."

That was it. I hit the point of information overload. "I'm done. I need to be alone." I got up from the table and returned to the guest room.

I jumped into the unfamiliar bed, jeans and all. Finally, much later than normal, it got dark outside and I fell asleep.

Chapter 13

I woke up early the next morning to the bright Alaska sun. I noticed for the first time thick black curtains could be drawn over the window to block the near constant offending summer daylight. It was only 4:30 A.M. Would have been nice if I'd noticed the darn curtains the night before.

I took my time getting ready for the day, carefully choosing a pair of jeans and nice shirt to wear. I spent extra time to blow dry my hair and apply what little makeup I had packed in the rush to leave Kansas.

I didn't care about my appearance today more than any other day. I was putting off the inevitable, facing the world downstairs and outside the cabin doors. Reality had become too strange for my liking.

Carmen was curled up on the couch downstairs, sipping a cup of coffee. "I'm sorry, did I wake you?"

"No, not at all. The very bright light woke me. What are you doing up?"

"My sensitivities make it hard for me to sleep when there is so much pain nearby."

"Wow. I'm not that pathetic, am I?"

She smiled at me. "Most certainly not. You've been through so much these past few days. There's some coffee in the kitchen. We have a variety of foods. Help yourself. This is your home for now. You may come and go as you please. Please be careful if you decide to go hiking. It's very easy to get lost and it's grizzly bear mating season. They're not so friendly to hikers."

I poured a large cup of coffee and then sat down on a poufy loveseat in the living room. "Thanks. You've been very kind. I'm sorry I haven't said it before. I'm just still in shock, I guess."

"It's a lot to take in. Hopefully when you meet the others, it will help you feel more at home. Konstantin wants to show you around, maybe meet some locals. I'll pick up a cell phone for you today so you can keep in touch with your family." She smiled into her cup. "You could call that young man you always think about."

"No, I can't."

"Why?" she asked. "Is there something I can do to help?"

"No." I took a sip of my coffee while I gathered my thoughts. "He saw me save the little girl. I hadn't discussed my ability with him before. I'm certain he never wants to see me again, after all the trouble I caused him."

"Well," she said, uncrossing her legs, "I never met the guy, but he must have cared for you. He instinctively protected you by releasing the statement. We didn't have anything to do with it."

Konstantin appeared, holding up a spatula, a wide grin on his face. "Who wants bacon and eggs, ladies?"

Carmen refocused briefly on me before turning to her husband. "Good morning to you, too. I'll take some."

"Aurora, how about some eggs?"

"Sure. Sounds great," I said.

After breakfast, Konstantin asked if I would be interested in a tour of the village. I threw on a light jacket and followed him out the door. I took a deep breath as soon we stepped outside. The air was cool and clean, with a freshness only pine trees and rain can bring.

The village was built on a small clearing at the base of a mountain. A paved road twisted through it. He led me about half a mile down the green hill toward the road. Houses and cabins dotted the foot of the mountain, some partially hidden by trees.

When we reached the road, brick buildings sat in a roughly straight line down what appeared to be 'the strip'. He pointed out one of them to me. "This is the library. It's huge. It has every kind of book you can imagine. We also order all the latest DVDs. You can just go in and take whatever you want and return it when you're done."

We continued our walk down the paved road that was most definitely the center of activity. My attention was drawn to a small café, where large groups of people clustered around the tables outside.

He led me to the cafe. A girl with super short, bright blond hair waved vigorously at us.

"You must be Aurora. My name is Julie. I'm so glad we have another flyer." She extended her hand and pumped mine enthusiastically. "How old are you? You look to be my age. I'm twenty-two."

I tried to follow her rapid fire style speech, but I was still stuck on the "flyer" lingo she had thrown out, and she reminded me of Bree. Ouch.

I shook off my discomfort and played nice as Konstantin introduced me to several other people.

After my face was sore from fake smiling, Konstantin touched my arm. "Want to go for a hike? I'd like to see what you can do, away from everyone."

"Sure," I said. "Can we invite Julie?"

"Yes. That's a nice idea. She's a strong flyer."

The trail we took twisted and turned up the mountain at a steep incline. The trees blocked out most of the light. The doom and gloom was starting to get to me, when the trees suddenly gave way to a long stretch of open, sunny, meadow dotted with only a few trees.

I put my face up to the sun and tried to soak it in, desperate to cleanse Gavyn from my brain. I put my hands out and pushed up my sleeves to get a little sun on my pale arms. I allowed myself to float up to the tops of the trees and out of the reach of the shadows.

Julie giggled and followed me up.

Konstantin joined us. "Okay. Let's see what you can do."

I looked up at the sun. I wanted to get closer to its cleansing light. Without saying another word, I shot toward the sky. I had never tried to go so fast before. The wind ripped through my hair, pulling out my ponytail holder. My light jacket flapped wildly in the wind created by my movement. It was exhilarating.

I looked down and saw Konstantin and Julie were far below, appearing only as small dots. I paused, enjoying the amazing view only I could see before heading back down.

"Holy crap!" Julie shouted as soon as I was close enough to hear. "Wicked! I've never seen anything like that!"

"Can you move horizontally as well as you move vertically?" Konstantin said.

"I think so."

"Okay. Let's go."

We skimmed along the top of the trees, slowly, so I could take in all the sights and sounds. Julie and Konstantin had to concentrate to move in the way I did. Their movements seemed sluggish next to mine. In a strange way, it made me feel good. It also made me feel weird. Not only was I a freak but I was a super freak.

Eventually, we landed just outside the village and walked back into the clearing. I went back to the cabin with Konstantin.

"You hungry?" he asked.

"Sure." I was never one to turn down food. He pulled some bread out of the cabinet and meat and cheese out of the fridge.

"Sandwiches okay? Carmen's the skilled cook around here."

"Perfect."

"So,"—he pulled open the bread and pulled out four slices—"you seem to have quite the ability. It's far above what I can do. Can you tell me about when you noticed you were different?"

"Yeah, I kinda noticed something was going on when I was reading in an armchair, looked down and saw I wasn't in the chair anymore, because I was floating above it."

"At least you were at home. How old were you?"

"14."

"Did you drop out of school?"

"No, why would I?"

He knitted his eyebrows together. "Because, until you learn to control it, it can be difficult to be in public."

"Oh. Yeah. I stayed home four weeks from school on a claim of Mono."

He dropped the bread he was holding and turned to face me. "Four weeks? That's all it took?"

"What, is that bad?" I asked.

He shook his head. "No, not bad. Good, different." He resumed his sandwich making.

"Christ, I am a freak." I slumped forward on the table, resting my head on my splayed out arms. "A freak that's been transplanted out of my pretend life into Alaska!"

He put a sandwich down in front of me. "You have lost a lot in this experience. I know you can never replace those friendships or experiences you've had, but please believe me, you will gain a million things with us. Carmen and I will do our best to look after you like you are our own."

Carmen breezed in the front door, shopping bags in hand. She pulled a compact black phone out of her back pocket and tossed it to me. "Here you go. Call your mom so she has your number. Please feel free to text and call at will. I also picked you up a few sweaters, but I'm not sure what you like. Maybe we can go shopping tomorrow to get you some more Alaska appropriate attire."

"Thanks," I said. "I feel bad just living off your charity. Maybe I can give you some money?"

"Don't worry about it. We won't take your money. Like I said, the organization owns some businesses, which earns us a nice income. We need to focus on educating you and keeping you safe."

After I finished my sandwich, I returned to the privacy of my room to call Mom with the new cell phone. She was slightly less angry and anxious.

I called Julie next, curious to see where our friendship would go. "Hey!" she said when I told her it was me calling. "I'm glad you called. I'll save your number. Why don't you come over to my cabin tonight? I'm having a few people over. We're just going to drink some beer and watch some movies."

"Sure. You can't go wrong with beer." I truly wanted to crawl into bed and cry for the rest of the night, but Julie's idea sounded more productive. Maybe the crowd of new people in my life would push out the memories of my former existence.

"Awesome. Come on over now. You can see my cabin from your dining room window. I'm the only one with my front door painted purple."

I paused by the front door as I left. "Hey, guys. Julie invited me over. I think I'm going to go."

"Great!" Carmen said. "Have fun. Go that way when you walk out, it's not far." She pointed to the wall behind her with her finger.

"Do I need a key?" I asked.

They looked at each other and laughed. "There are no locks. There is no danger here," Carmen said.

"Oh, right."

I walked in the direction Carmen pointed, looking for a cabin with a purple door. It wasn't hard to spot. It was tiny, built with dark wood, and nestled in the trees. An old wooden table and chair set crowded the small porch. Brightly colored blankets thrown over the railing waved gently in the breeze like Tibetan prayer flags. Julie and two people around my age had beers and were relaxing in the chairs.

Julie waved me over to the porch.

"Hey, Aurora, this is Karen." She gestured at the tall, thin, attractive brunette with striking blue eyes.

Karen shook my hand. "Nice to meet you. It's good to have a fellow Texan around. I'm from Gonzales, Texas."

"And this is Damien."

He unfolded his considerable length while he stood to shake my hand. He was handsome with chiseled features and long dreadlocks. "Would you like a beer?" he asked.

"Sure."

He reached a giant muscular arm behind him and retrieved one from the cooler. "So," he said, "you're a flyer? From what Julie said, you're really good."

"Oh. Yeah. I guess I am a flyer. What about you, Damien?" Apparently, superhuman abilities were a casual topic of conversation around here.

"I'm what they call a blocker. Has Carmen or Konstantin explained blockers to you yet?"

"Briefly."

"Well, I travel with those two a lot. I'm useful to have around when dealing with them."

Them. I needed to learn more about them. I opened my mouth to ask Damien, but Julie interrupted. "We're all more than just our gifts. Why don't you tell us more about you?"

"I was in law school before I came here. My mom and my sister live in Kansas, which is where I lived for a long time. Parents divorced when I was two and my dad is not in the picture. That's about it. I'm boring."

"Law school?" Damien asked. "That's not boring. That's pretty cool, actually. I always thought I would go to law school and be a district attorney."

"Why don't you?" I asked.

"Tuition, time, and I've got this, which is way more fun."

Karen was quiet during the conversation. I turned my attention to her. "So, Karen. What's your gig?"

She laughed. "Well, I'm not one of the talented kids. I'm Damien's handler," she said.

Julie opened her front door. "Hey, you guys want to watch the movie?"

"Sure," I said.

During the movie, I saw the images move across the screen, but I didn't comprehend the movie. My mind was a million miles away. I tried to reconcile all of this new information with my life. I felt the pull of my old life, of him. I wanted to hear his voice so badly.

The cell phone was heavy in my pocket, but I resisted the urge to dial the numbers I knew so well.

After the movie, I bade my new friends a good night before walking out into the still light late evening. I enjoyed the brief walk back to my temporary home. Back in my bedroom, I drew the black curtains shut to block out the sun. I changed into pajamas, jumped into bed, and scrunched my eyes shut, trying to block the thoughts of Gavyn, Mom, Erica, my friends, and even my familiar apartment in San Antonio that was mine no longer.

I was not successful.

Chapter 14

The café was crowded today as usual. Konstantin walked quickly ahead of me, having dragged me out of bed early for some reason.

Ugh. This was the new nexus of my social life.

A stocky middle aged man with shaved head and deep tan stood as we approached. Something about him screamed military. Several somethings about him actually. His movements were smooth, controlled, and precise, with his eyes constantly darting around to take in his surroundings. He was dressed in boots and rugged pants.

"Good morning, Konstantin," he said in a British accent. I thought of Gavyn and his British accent, and his perfect eyes, and…

"I'm Dennis. Konstantin has told me all about you. I'm very glad to meet you."

I shook his hand. "Nice to meet you."

"Dennis has come in for a visit from one of our groups in England. He's going to be coming with us today," Konstantin said.

"Okie dokie."

Two miles in a strictly upward motion in a thick forest landed us in a large open clearing ringed by trees. My thighs ached with effort and I had sweated so much I was 90% sure I had pit marks. Dennis wasn't even out of breath from the vigorous hike.

"Dennis is, you could say, a type of blocker. He can't fly. But please, show him what you showed me yesterday," Konstantin said.

"Okay." I zipped up my jacket to defend against the cold air, took a deep breath, and flew. I rose to the top of the trees and paused, waiting for further instruction from Konstantin.

"Fast, like you did yesterday," Konstantin yelled from the ground.

It was new for me, to have complete freedom to move. The air moved around and through me. Surges of energy rolled through my body. I rocketed through the air, even faster than before. My futile ponytail holder flew out of my hair. I felt like I could go forever and ever. I stopped when I realized I was very, very cold. I swallowed my panic when I looked down. I had gone too far. I couldn't tell where I had come from.

Thankfully, I saw a small dot moving above green blobs of trees below. I surged down toward the dot. Konstantin met me halfway. "Nice."

We returned to solid ground, where Dennis was still waiting and watching. "Wow. Impressive," he said. "You're very good."

"So I passed my demonstration? Do I get a sticker?"

Dennis smiled. "I heard you are a sharp little thing."

"I'm not a 'little thing'. "

"My apologies. I didn't mean any offense."

"Let's go back," Konstantin said. "You look tired."

"Sure."

Dennis fell into step next to me as we hiked back to the village. "Please tell me, how did you learn to control your ability on your own?"

"I wasn't on my own. My mom helped me. I would practice all day at not floating away. I stood in front of her in the kitchen and tried over and over until I got it right. I'm still not sure how I do it."

"Sounds about right. I think of it as kind of like pissing."

Now it was my turn to laugh. "Pissing?"

"Yes, pissing. You don't have to actively think about not pissing your pants, but you are holding in your piss almost constantly."

"I guess that's true."

"What do you do when you are not flying?" he asked. "It looks like you work out. Do you?"

"Yes, well no. Kind of. Until a short while ago, I used to run a lot, and lift weights."

"You should keep up your fitness while you are here. Hike outside while you can. It will get much, much colder."

As we approached the clearing near the cabins, both men were quiet.

"Aurora, why don't you get something to eat?" Konstantin said, motioning to the direction of his cabin. "I think Carmen mentioned shopping with you today. Dennis and I need to speak in private."

"Oh, okay. You need to talk about me. Go for it." On a crazy impulse, I hugged Konstantin. He seemed surprised, but pleased. I offered my hand to Dennis. "It was nice to meet you."

"The pleasure was all mine. You are an amazing girl, and not just because of what you can do." His giant leathery hand wrapped around mine briefly.

I took my time walking back to the cabin. Carmen was pulling a meatloaf out of the oven. "Perfect timing. I was hoping we could eat and then drive into town to shop this afternoon. Maybe you can invite Julie?"

An hour later I was in the Jeep with Julie and Carmen, headed to Fairbanks to get new clothes. I looked at the cold rural surroundings, doubtful of what kind of shopping we could do here.

"So, who is Dennis exactly?"

"He's one of the leaders in our society. He heads up one of the divisions. We'll talk about it more later." She glanced at Julie in the back seat as she spoke.

"Sure, whatever." I craned my head to look at Julie. "How is it you came to be here?"

She closed her compact and shoved it in her purse before answering. "I came here when I was nineteen. My great grandfather had the same ability. He watched me until it became active and then introduced me to the others and this life. He lives in Montana. He left a couple of years ago when he was sure I'd be okay on my own up here."

"Are you here alone?" I asked. "I mean, do you have any family here?"

"Yes. I'm here alone, in the sense my family isn't here. But I have close friends here and it feels like family. I'm working at the bookstore in our village part time, and doing online classes so I can finish my bachelors."

"Oh. Why don't you go to college in Fairbanks?" I asked.

She sighed. "The same reason you couldn't do it either. I don't have a handler yet. I venture out into the world a little bit, because that's how you meet your handler, but I have to be careful."

"Oh."

We went to a small mall in Fairbanks. Despite my general depression, it was fun to shop with the girls. For the first time since I arrived in Alaska, laughter came naturally.

I counted no less than seven shopping bags in my hands as we walked back to the car after a three hour marathon shopping session. I was the proud owner several pairs of thermal lined jeans, long sleeved shirts, knit caps, sneakers and hiking boots.

On our way back, Carmen uttered a low oath and swerved the car into a strip mall. "Almost forgot!"

"Me too!" said Julie.

I leaned forward so I could read the sign of the store. "Ice cream?"

"You bet. We have to eat it now, while it's summer. Trust me, you won't want to eat it when it gets to twenty below with the wind chill," Julie answered. "And it's a long, long winter here."

Back at the cabin, Julie hopped out of the car and gave me a quick hug. "See you later."

Inside, Konstantin and Dennis were sitting at the dining table. Several small white take-out boxes were in front of them.

"We have much to discuss," Dennis said in a formal tone. "Do you like Chinese? We drove to Fairbanks just to get it."

"Okay. Sounds good," I said.

Tension crackled in the air. I put the shopping bags in my room and ran a brush through my unruly hair before returning downstairs.

Carmen spread out paper plates on the table and grabbed forks and spoons for everyone. I eagerly dug into the spicy food. It was the worse Chinese food I had ever eaten, but it was perfect after the cool ice cream snack. It was mostly silent while we ate. Everyone, including me, was waiting for something to happen. I finished my food and was examining the patterns in the wood on the table when Dennis's clipped voice broke my train of thought.

"Thanks for letting me tag along today. I'm sure you noticed I was watching you very carefully."

"Everyone stares at the circus freak."

He pushed his food around his plate. "Did Carmen or Konstantin tell you anything about me?"

I looked at Carmen. She nodded. "Well, yeah. Carmen said you were big dog in the organization. I'm sure you're getting ready to tell me more?"

"Yes, but first let's talk about you." He leaned forward on the table, pushed his plate away, and folded his arms in front of him. "I'm a completely honest person. I have a feeling you are the same way. So, I'm going to be blunt with you. I think it's only fair for someone in your situation."

"Got it. Go."

"I'm ninety-seven years old, and I have been with the organization since I was a teenager. I have never seen any flying ability like yours before. Period."

"You're ninety-seven?" I said. "For reals?"

His face pulled into a smile, making the skin around his eyes crinkle. Even so, he didn't look a day over a very fit fifty. "Yes. We age slower, but this is about you, not me. Aurora, you're fast. You have complete control over your gift. Most people have years of practice and training before they can return to society to live normally, if they so choose. You have been able to do it without any help. You picked up everything

Konstantin showed you instantly. I can't imagine the true extent of your ability. It's amazing, really."

He looked at Konstantin before continuing. "Konstantin and I both agree your abilities are phenomenal. You could be of great asset to the organization. We just disagree on how best to utilize you, for now at least."

"Damn right, we do," Konstantin said. "I need you to understand something very important. Whatever you decide to do, whether it is to work with the organization or return to normal society, it's your decision." He smoothed his face back into calm composure. "Go on, Dennis, tell her. She needs to know anyway."

My eyes darted back and forth between Konstantin and stoic Dennis.

"How much do you know about them? The ones who chase us?" Dennis asked.

"Not much because you guys haven't told me jack," I said. "I know they hunt us. I know they were tracking me, which is why I came here."

"Here's your 101. We call them Shyama, a Hindi word for 'dark ones.' Their sole purpose is to destroy those with abilities. We don't know where they came from, but they've been around as long as we have." He paused, glancing at Carmen and Konstantin. "They usually take a human form."

I rubbed my forehead with one hands desperately trying to figure out where this new information would fit into reality. "What do you mean? What other form do they take?"

Konstantin covered my free hand with his. "It's okay. You're safe here. We don't know a lot about what exactly they are, but we will tell you everything we know. Okay?" He patted my hand before pulling it back, and then looked at Dennis.

"It's true," Dennis said. "We don't know exactly what they are. I'm not sure classifying them would help you understand.

"Here's what we do know. We think there are four or five thousand worldwide, give or take a few. They don't age, and they don't die, except under very specific instances. They can take on many forms and move rapidly from on place to another, almost like teleportation.

"The only thing that seems to really trip them up is a handler. They appear to be able to monitor media outlets on some level, and look for leaks like yours. Sometimes, they figure out who the identities of families of the gifted ones are and, well, go after them."

"What about my family? Couldn't they figure it out and go after them?" I said.

"Your family is fine," Konstantin said. "We have blockers there watching over them."

"Why? Why do they do this?" I asked. "What are these things?"

"I wish we knew what they are exactly. That's why we work so hard to find those with abilities. If they find you first, well, let's just say a lot of people die." His voice was thick. He paused, taking a swig of his beer. "There's more, if you are ready," he said, glancing at Konstantin.

"Oh, man." I drained my wineglass. "Any more shocking bad news?" Life was darker, now and I was afraid of the how much darker it would get.

"I'm telling you all of this for a reason. The division I head up is essentially tactical offense. Rather than passively waiting for them to find us and defend our brothers and sisters, we go after them." He sat up taller. "We draw them out and attack, taking them down one by one. I'd like you to join us."

My head reeled again. I placed my hand on the table, just to feel something solid. "Join...us?"

He smiled. "Yes. Fight back."

Carmen spoke. "There are many paths. You don't have to take this one, and you don't have to decide now. It's an option. That's all." She directed her words at me, but her bright eyes bore into Dennis as she spoke.

"Jesus Christ. What sort of crazy ass crap have I gotten myself into?" I tilted my head back until I found my voice again. "What would this entail for me?"

Dennis answered. "It means you would train here with us for a while. Then you would join operations."

"Oh." A dead silence followed my words. A clock ticked, the trees outside brushed against the wall, and a bird chirped in the distance. I grabbed my beer and paced over to the living room window.

I was part of a secret war the world did not know about, a war I had no choice but to fight. The furious pace of my mind gave way to numbness. I thought of family, friends, and Gavyn. Their faces flashed behind my closed eyes, playing a movie of a life that didn't belong to me anymore. I was a menace to everyone I loved. Wherever I went they would follow, destroying everyone.

But I understood now. My life as a normal person was over. I would never get married, never have children, and never finish school. I had a new life here, and I needed to accept it. I had to cut the chord of hope connecting me to my old life and to Gavyn.

My stupid self replayed our story over and over in my head. I remembered everything; the first time I met him, his handsome features, the way his scent filled me up when we were tangled together, and his gentle but urgent touch. A memory of a life I almost had but would never be mine.

A million miles away from my focus, Konstantin got up from the table. Carmen put a hand on his arm, gently pulling him back to his seat. "Leave her be. She's okay. She's figuring it out."

I stared out the window for what felt like hours. Surely, with time, I would be all right. A new direction would help me move on, literally and figuratively.

Then I was done thinking and ready for action. I had no choice. I returned to the table, where they still sat in quiet conversation.

"I'm in."

Chapter 15

"Eight fifteen, Aurora. Pick it up!" Konstantin shouted. He tapped his watch as I ran by. "You're slowing down."

I grunted in response. It was all I could do at mile six. I'd been up since 4:30, and I was tired. Nevertheless, I pushed forward. Sooner than I thought, I looped around the thick trees to return to Konstantin at the edge of the forest.

"Seven thirty. Good girl," he said as I sailed past him. I slowed down to a walk as we passed into the clearing that housed our village.

He handed me a bottle of water as we walked home. "You're getting faster. Not bad for ten weeks of training."

I gulped down half the bottle before I answered. "Not bad? I thought I was kind of bad-ass, actually."

He smiled. "Like I said, not bad."

Dennis was sitting at the kitchen table with a cup off coffee when we came in. "How far?" he said.

"Seven," Konstantin said. "Average seven forty-five splits."

"Oh, not bad," Dennis said. "Rinse off, we need to get a move on."

"Oh, please. Don't get too heavy with the praise."

Dennis tossed me a smile. Turns out the old bear did have a tiny sense of humor.

Carmen appeared at my shoulder. "That's man-speak for good." She squeezed my elbow. "And you're not going anywhere until you get a full meal."

She made a full spread: eggs, bacon, chopped cantaloupe, coffee and water. Dennis ate quickly, then stared at me while I ate.

"Stop it!" I told him through a mouthful eggs. "It's creepy."

"We need to get moving," he said.

"Fine." I shoved my plate away, wiped my mouth, and stood. He was already holding the front door for me.

He led me to the forest in his fast gait. He was in his usual attire, some sort of militaryish cargo pants and heavy sweater.

I ran a few steps to catch up to him. "So what's today? Knife fighting? Jujitsu? Firearms?"

"Firearms." He didn't bother to look at me while we talked.

"Oh."

This time he glanced at me. "You sound disappointed."

"No, not really, but knife fighting is fun. It makes me feel like a super secret ninja," I said.

"Super secret ninja? What is this?"

"Never mind." I kicked the dirt as we approached the shooting range housed in a long, narrow clearing in the forest. "Old man," I muttered.

"Heard that. Use your subcompact today." He pointed at the hard black box containing my gun.

I flipped open the latches on the box. "But I like big guns. What about an AR-15?"

"You can carry a subcompact with you wherever you go. The Shyama will follow you wherever you go. You can't carry an AR-15 with you when you go grocery shopping, but you can carry a sub, so we focus on the sub. Got it?"

"I could totally get an AR-15 to the grocery store. Have you seen my purse collection?"

He rolled his eyes. "Gun, Aurora. Pick up the damn gun."

Oopsie. Now he looked angry. I picked up the gun and shoved in the clip. I put on my ear protection and looked behind me to make sure Dennis had his on too. Then, I shot in rapid succession until the clip was empty. When the dust cleared, the center of the target was in tatters.

He smiled. "Good."

By the time I got back to the cabin, dusk had arrived. I showered and found Carmen on the front porch, wrapped in a quilt to block the cold air.

"Where is Dennis?" I said.

"He went back to his place. Konstantin went with him."

"Oh."

She patted the seat next to me. "Sit."

We swung back and forth. "Your new passports arrived today," she said.

"Which ones?" I asked.

She grinned. "UK, Sweden, and South Africa."

"I don't even want to know how you get forged passports," I said.

"They're not forged. They are real government issued documents with your real name, picture and address. The fake names and addresses come later. Having a 140 year life span can complicate things for you. Aurora Lockette will eventually need to die, at least in name, so you can get a new SSN number."

"I hadn't even thought of that," I said. "This is still so weird. This big secret, all of us."

"You'll get used to it. The tough part comes later."

"How so?"

"When you meet someone special. When you want to get married. That will probably be the next person you tell. And then later, your kids. They'll notice you're not aging normally at some point. No one else can know, really."

I laughed, but it came out forced. "I'm currently stuck on someone I can't have and even if I wasn't, how the hell am I supposed to find love when the Shyama are hunting me down? How am I supposed to be with someone who gets older and ages and gets sick, when I don't? I don't see it Carmen. I just don't."

"Your time will come."

I narrowed my eyes at her. "What is it?"

"I can tell your still struggling with him." She looked at me with pity in her bright aqua eyes.

It was true, of course. I was pathetic. The hole in my heart was not healing with time as conventional wisdom had promised.

Three months had passed since I'd fled to Alaska. I was patient, waiting for the new activities that consumed my day to distract me, waiting for good old father time to at least lessen the tightness in my chest. But it didn't. I was still in love with Gavyn. Hopelessly, foolishly in love.

"I don't know what the hell to do with myself sometimes, but I'm trying to get out there and be normal. At least as normal as I can be, seeing as how I am some sort of super-freak living in a village full of super-freaks and being hunted by dark forces."

She leaned her head against me and threw some of her quilt over my legs. "You do try hard. It's difficult to watch sometimes. Why don't you call him? You need to ask what he actually thinks before you shut him out forever."

"In the unlikely event he would want to talk to me, I can't do that to him. I can't put him in danger."

"Calling him won't put him in danger," she reminded me.

"No." My voice dropped a whisper. "I can't hear his voice and not see him." I pulled the blanket to cover more of my body. "This way is better. I'm okay. Don't worry."

She stood. "Don't be a foolish girl. Life is too short." She tugged on the corner of the quilt. "Are you going to stay out here?"

I stood. "Nope. I'm cold, and I still smell like gunpowder."

I followed her into the house.

"Help me with dinner?" she asked.

"Sure." I washed my hands, rubbing the soap all the way to my elbow. I had flat calluses forming where the hot gun touched my skin, round after round. It was one more sign I was morphing into a different person. My body was hardened with compact muscle, my gait was fast and strong.

I could fight. I could kill. I could win.

I still couldn't cook worth a damn though so I chopped vegetables and grated cheese for the tacos. Carmen did everything else. She pulled them out of the oven as Konstantin and Dennis walked in the front door.

"Good timing," Carmen said. She saw their faces and her tone changed. "What's up?"

Dennis plopped down at the kitchen table. "We have some activity we need to address."

I followed Carmen to the table with a stack of plates. She served the greasy tacos with a giant spatula. Dennis waited until we had time to eat at least some of our food before he spoke again.

"A situation has come to my attention."

Carmen spoke next. "Where?"

"New Orleans. There is a group of us there. They have four blockers out there, but something is off. One of the females, Maryanna, is having problems. She has seen the Shyama three times now. She has a handler, but I think something must be wrong with the bond. We need to evacuate them. This is an excellent opportunity for us."

"How many Shyama are there?" Konstantin asked.

"Just two, as far as we can tell."

Carmen threw her napkin on the table. "You want to take Aurora, don't you? Use her to draw them out?"

"Yes," Dennis answered. "We'll take a good team. She's unbonded, so she can easily draw them out with her presence and see how we operate. It'll be a good learning experience for her."

"I don't like this," Konstantin said.

"You can't keep her in here forever. She needs to find a handler."

"He's right," I said. "Like it or not, I'm a target and I need to see how this works. This is what I've been training for." My heart was pounding and my palms were a little sweaty, but not from fear. I was excited.

Dennis smiled. "We move out in two days. We'll be taking all of you, plus Damien and Karen. We'll all fly. Oh, on a plane, I mean." He winked at me. "My brother will meet you at the airport. We have four blockers from Houston meeting us there. They will drive in with the weapons."

"Why is your brother meeting us there?" I asked.

"He's my handler. His name is Ben, you'll like him." He stood to leave. "I must go. There is much to do." Konstantin followed him out.

I was alone with Carmen in the kitchen. She leaned against the counter and folded her petite arms over her chest. "Why are you so excited? I feel off about this."

"Yeah. Something is definitely off. I can fly, you can read minds, and we're being hunted."

She gave me a look I'd seen on my mother's face before, a mixture of amusement, anger, and reproach. "You didn't answer my question. You should be a little afraid, at least."

"Well, I've been trained to do this, right? I'll get scared later," I said.

"You're reckless. It all boils down to him, doesn't it? You need to resolve your feelings for him. This is not healthy."

"Can I not have any privacy here? Even inside my head?" I ran up to my room and slammed the door behind me.

I was wrong to snap at her. She'd been taking care of me for months now. I rocked slowly in the chair beside the window, staring out into the dark, snowy, world outside. I couldn't see much, but my mind welcomed the view nonetheless. I switched on the lamp beside me and read a novel, grasping for the distraction I knew wouldn't work.

The next morning, I woke up to the sweet smell of pancakes and bacon wafting through the cabin. I pulled on a thick robe and slippers and went downstairs, my stomach rumbling with hunger.

"Good morning," Carmen said, still in her pajamas like me. "Do you want some breakfast?"

"Yeah."

She piled a plate with pancakes, syrup and bacon burned to a crisp, just the way I liked it.

I took the plate from her and set it down on the counter behind me. "Look, I'm a turd," I said. "I'm sorry I snapped at you last night. I really appreciate all you've done for me. I want you to know that."

She embraced me, rubbing my back soothingly. "I shouldn't have said what I did. It's not my place to comment on him."

We ate breakfast together at the table, our conversation tuned to a much lighter note.

"Hey, I was thinking. Why don't we head into town with Julie and have some fun? We can get our hair done or go shopping or anything you want. It would be nice to try and relax before we leave tomorrow," she said as she pushed her now empty plate away from her.

"Cool. I'll call Julie."

Julie, of course, immediately agreed to come. She suggested pedicures, an idea I latched onto.

I got ready quickly, eager to get into town and come back for our meeting. As I was blow drying my hair, a flick of movement on my wrist caught my eye. It was the bracelet Gavyn had given me. I stared at it for long time, wondering how I could have possibly forgotten I had it on.

It was a shackle, tying me to something that wasn't mine. I yanked at it roughly, trying to pull it over my hand. It was snug around my wrist, just as Gavyn had tied it. I wanted it gone. Now. I rummaged through my drawer looking for a pair of scissors.

Carmen's voice floated up the stairs. "Aurora? You ready? Julie's here, hon."

I slammed the scissors down and grabbed my purse. Bracelet intact, I pasted a big fake smile on my face before heading downstairs.

It was the dead of winter, but it was always winter in Alaska. The ground was covered with ice and snow, the trees marked with white frosting. When I paid attention, the beauty of this place was breathtaking.

We pulled up to the salon several minutes later. It was pretty, with soft eggshell green décor. Fortunately for us, it was also very warm. We eagerly took off our snow boots and climbed into the chairs, dipping our feet in the bubbling water. After a few minutes of pampering, my body relaxed.

Carmen had her eyes closed and was leaning back in her chair. Julie, for once, did not feel the need to talk and was sitting silently as she flipped through a magazine. I grabbed a magazine off the rack next to me. Girly nonsense was the theme of the day, after all.

"Sexy Brit star woes onset love interest," the headline blared. The paparazzi style picture showed Gavyn, looking just as handsome and perfect as I remembered him. His arm was casually slung over the shoulder of Mira Tavana, his breathtaking costar in *Blue Leaf*. The caption indicated the photograph was taken outside a restaurant in L.A.

The surprising pain ripped through my thin facade. I tried to fight it off, but it consumed me. I was still sitting in silence as I stared at the page that had just shattered the little sanity I had left.

Carmen's eyes popped open and she shot up in her chair, instantly alerted to my state of mind. "What is it?" she whispered, flicking her red hair out her face as she spoke. Her eyes darted down to the magazine splayed across my lap. "Oh." She took the magazine off my lap, re-shelving it quickly.

Of course he had moved on. Why wouldn't he? Why would he worry about me when he could have someone like Mira?

Carmen leaned forward and whispered in my ear. "I'm sorry. That's not something you should have to see." I glanced over at Julie, who was now watching my sudden outburst with concern.

"I'm okay," I managed to say, my voice thick with repressed tears. "I'm okay," I repeated. I leaned back in my chair and closed my eyes. I took deep breath, counting to five to inhale and five to exhale. It was all I could do to keep from becoming completely unglued. Behind my eyes, the picture of the happy couple was burned on my retina.

Somehow, despite all my denials to Carmen and myself, I had clung to a fantasy. I hid a small glimmer of hope deep inside my being that Gavyn still loved me, that he wasn't afraid of me, that he wanted to be with me.

Julie's concerned voice worked on the edge of my conscience, sounding like it was far off in the distance. "What's wrong? Are you sick?"

"She'll be okay. She saw something that upset her," Carmen said.

I sat very still, waiting to calm down. Eventually, the pain started to fade into something else. Something hard. Something angry. I could hear the bubble of the pedicure baths and the soft chatter of the technicians. I was present again. I opened my eyes, determined to fake it.

I spent the rest of day in almost complete silence. Julie was kind enough to fill my silence with her chatter. Carmen watched me, but said little as we moved through the shopping mall and off to an Italian restaurant for lunch.

Back at the cabin, Dennis gathered everyone and spread out maps of the Garden District and the French Quarter of New Orleans on the table. "Study it and memorize all the streets. We'll be doing this at night, so we can't have any confusion. Understand?"

We all nodded in response.

"The group coven lives here." He put his finger down on the map. "The Shyama have been spotted here, here, and here." His fingers moved to three locations on the map, all in the heart of the French quarter.

He pulled a marker out of his pocket and circled a small swatch of land off the Mississippi river, only a few blocks away from Jackson Square. "This is tricky, because it's in a touristy area. It's the dead of winter, so it won't be too crowded. There's lots of tall grass here. It will block us off visually from the city, plus the river is right there to dispose of the remains. We all hide here, except for Aurora. Your job is to draw them out, have them follow you to this location."

"Yes, sir."

"You will all have your usual weapons. For our new girl,"—he paused and nudged my shoulder playfully—"that means I want you to have two guns."

"Yeah, I know. A semi-auto as my primary, a small revolver as a secondary," I finished for him.

"And a knife," he said. "You've had enough training to handle it. Wear it on your torso."

By the time I went upstairs to finish packing, it was 1:00 A.M. I crawled into bed, exhausted and dreading the early alarm I needed to get to the airport in time. I closed my eyes and tried to review the mission information one more time in my mind. Of course, my brain disobeyed my commands and returned to the painful image I saw in the magazine.

I gave up and stayed awake until it was time to leave for the airport.

Chapter 16

I slept fitfully the entire way to Seattle, nodding in and out of consciousness during the long flight. From Seattle to Orleans I was wide awake.

Konstantin sat next to me in the plane, Carmen on his other side.

"Welcome back," he joked. "Feel the adrenalin? You probably won't sleep much from here on out."

"True story. I'm wired."

"Don't worry. You'll be safe. The blockers from Houston have already checked into the hotel."

"Thanks. I feel okay about it." It was true. I wasn't afraid. I didn't feel anything really, just kind of dead and numb inside. I'm pretty sure that was a bad thing, but I was okay with it anyway.

By the time we landed in New Orleans, night had fallen. We drove through the dark streets of the city still bearing the visible scars of Hurricane Katrina. The highway twisted by the eerie above ground mausoleums.

"Why are graveyards like that?"

"They've tried to bury their dead here before, but the soil is too swampy and they wouldn't stay buried. After a heavy rain, bodies would become unearthed and float down the streets," Carmen said.

"Oh, wow."

The French Quarter wore a different dress than the rest of the city. The narrow one-way streets were marked by the courtyard style buildings with their balconies overlooking the street. As expected, there were plenty of people walking around, toting their drinks.

The hotel was located on Bourbon Street, smack in the middle of the action. In another setting, it would have been the perfect place to stay and live it up. The historic building had a pretty façade with green iron balconies. The inside lobby was furnished with cream-colored furniture.

I was sharing a room with Konstantin and Carmen. I thought it was odd, but said nothing. The room was connected by a door to a suite on either side. The blockers were staying in the adjoining suites, creating a mini-wall of protection around me.

I sank onto one of the soft queen beds. There used to be a time when I could travel without a posse of blockers to protect me from a sinister force.

Carmen sat on the other bed in silence, her red hair forming a curtain around her face. She had her eyes closed and her chin was dropped to her chest. I learned to leave her alone when she was doing this. After a few minutes passed by, she opened her eyes and tilted her head side-to-side, stretching out her neck.

"Well?" Konstantin asked, walking out of the restroom. He sat by his wife, rubbing her shoulder.

"They can sense we are here, but they have no idea where. They won't be able to get a fix on Aurora while we are all with her. It's working."

There was soft knock on the door. Konstantin let Dennis in and updated him.

"Excellent." He walked into the room and folded his arms across his chest, all business. "The locals are staying inside their home nearby until they get a signal from us. Once we give them the all clear, they are going straight to the airport. Me, Ben, Damien and Karen are two doors down from here, in another suite like this one."

He stood near the window, gazing outside, hands crossed behind his back. "We'll do surveillance tomorrow to see if we can pinpoint them. Aurora will stay here with the blockers. If all goes well, tomorrow night we make our move."

We all nodded solemnly.

"Against my better judgment, I suggest we all go out for dinner, together." He gestured to the rooms on either side with a quick nod.

"Oh, if it's easier, I can just stay behind."

"No. You must go where the blockers go, and they need to eat too. Plus, you need to get out. How else are you going to meet your handler?" Dennis asked.

Dinner was in a hole in the wall Cajun place with live Zydeco music. The mood was cheerful, but still subdued. We were there on serious business. No one touched a drop of alcohol.

Hours passed back in the room. It was dark, the TV was off and Carmen and Konstantin were asleep, but I wasn't. Sounds floated through the window: music and the occasional drunken yell or car horn.

I must have drifted off at some point because the next morning, Carmen shook me awake. She was already dressed. "We're getting ready to leave. Get up in case we need you."

As soon as the door closed behind me I jumped up and got in the shower, relieved I could at least do that in private. I glanced at the doors leading to the adjoining suites, wondering what the blockers were doing.

I dressed quickly and brushed out my hair. It tumbled down to my waist now. My arms and shoulders were clearly defined with compact muscle. My eyes were different too. Sad.

I gave up on my reflection and entertained myself by staring out the window. It was 9:30 in the morning and some very intense tourists were already walking around with the famous hand grenade drinks. I entertained myself by imagining what their individual lives must be like, inventing identities and dramas in my head. I envied them and their simple, Shyama free lives.

Keith, the blocker from Houston I had met the night before, knocked on my door. He was tall and muscular with a shock of auburn hair. "Hey, I thought you might be hungry." He handed me a plastic wrapped sandwich. He plopped himself on my bed and flipped on the T.V.

"Thanks, Keith. Make yourself at home."

"Will do." He smiled, which made me notice he was damn hot.

We ate in comfortable silence, watching a stupid comedy on the television. I was relaxing and doing nothing, but I knew he was active as he used his ability to protect me. I let my mind remain blank, refusing to visit the dark parts today.

Carmen and Konstantin returned late in the afternoon.

"What's the latest?" Keith asked as soon as they walked in.

"We didn't see them. We need to draw them closer. Aurora, let's go. You're up," Konstantin said. "You're just going to walk around with me and Carmen, like a normal tourist. If I say go, run. We need to get them down to this neighborhood."

I grabbed my purse. "Wait," Konstantin said. He walked to the bathroom and returned with a gun and a holster for my pants pocket. "You must always arm yourself when they are close like this."

I put the holster in my pocket and tugged my bulky sweater over it. "Okay. I'm ready."

We walked out into the breezy bright afternoon. Tourists were bundled up in jackets, but we were comfortable in our sweaters. This was almost tropically warm to us Alaskans. We walked from store to store in the French Quarter. Out of the corner of my eye, I spotted familiar faces in the crowd. I saw Dennis once and Damien twice.

We made our way down to Jackson Square. I was admiring the small artist booths set up on the perimeter, when Carmen grabbed my arm, stopping me in my tracks. "Go. Now!" She roughly spun me in the direction of the hotel.

I sped walked, weaving my way through the packed crowd. I was afraid of drawing too much attention to myself. Out of nowhere, Damien appeared at my shoulder, winding his arm through the crook of my elbow.

"Run," he said in my ear, then loosened his grip and gave me a gentle push.

I felt the tiniest stab of fear as I jogged back to the hotel. I glanced at my side and saw I was now trailed by Karen, as well as Damien. "Faster!" Damien shouted, not bothering to be discreet.

I broke into a dead sprint to the lobby of the hotel. Damien appeared at my elbow and guided me to the stairs as soon as I came through the doors. The four blockers were waiting outside my hotel room. They opened the door and pulled me in as soon as I was within grabbing distance.

Damien and Karen came through the door a second later. Karen whipped out her gun and stationed herself next to the door. Damien pulled out a large firearm, slammed the magazine into the bottom of the gun and pulled the slide in one smooth movement. He stood in front of the four trackers, facing the hotel door.

I sat very still on the floor where Keith had shoved me as soon as I came in. Now, the fear was clear, the cobwebs of numbness wiped out of my brain.

Tension tightened the air. Two taps made us all jump. "It's Carmen, let me in." Karen threw open the door, not lowering her firearm.

Carmen came in, Konstantin behind her. "They didn't see her. Thank God. They're on this block, but they can't tell which hotel we are in." She was breathless as she spoke, her fingers tightly wound with Konstantin's. "That was close."

Karen pulled a chair up to the door and sat down. Damien sat too, keeping his firearm in his hand. "How did they get so damn close without us knowing?"

"I don't know. They usually don't go near crowds like the one in Jackson Square." Her voice trailed off. "I'm sorry, Aurora. For a second there, they were closing in on you."

"Don't we want them around here so they'll follow us to the river?" I asked, keeping my voice detached and steady. It frightened me to run away from something without knowing exactly what it was.

"Yes," Konstantin answered me. "You did well." He turned to Carmen, putting his hand on her face. It was an intimate gesture that made me look away. "Carmen, what's going on? Are you okay? They were really close before you saw them."

"There's a distraction at the perimeter of my thoughts. I can't put my finger on it." She placed her hand on top of his. "I won't let it happen again. They'll be here when Aurora leads them to the river."

Awkward didn't even begin to describe the rest of the afternoon. Afraid to leave me alone, the blockers stayed in the room. Karen and Damien eventually moved into an adjoining suite to watch television, but they left the shared door open and their firearms in easy reach.

I reclined on my bed. I tried to ignore the two blockers sitting at the foot of my bed, but was unsuccessful. Maybe under different circumstances it would be nice to have two good-looking, brawny guys in my hotel room.

And boy, did I notice them. Especially Keith. He was handsome in a generic, all American sort of way. I admired his bulging biceps from my vantage point. I had been so out of it yesterday I failed to notice his assets at dinner the night before.

Carmen shot me a glance out of the corner of her eye with a small smile. I smiled back. I was glad we could share the secret without saying a word, though I was embarrassed to be caught with less than pure thoughts.

We ordered room service for dinner and ate in silence. The blockers were concentrating and no one wanted to distract them.

After dinner, I plopped on the bed and stared at the ceiling. To my surprise, Keith re-seated himself on the bed right next to me. He briefly pressed the outside of his hand gently on my cheek.

"You feel a little warm. You okay?" he asked.

"I'm okay." There was the tiniest of sparks with his touch. "I think I'm just a little freaked out by all this."

"Okay. Try and get some rest. You're on next. I won't let anything happen to you." He scooted back down to the foot of my bed, next to the other blocker.

The hours dragged on. There was no rest, just the passage of time.

"It's time," Konstantin said.

Adrenaline moved through my body, setting every nerve ending on fire. I glanced at the beside clock; 1:55 in the early morning.

The room was a flurry of activity. Damien pulled a large machete out of a protective sheath and examined it briefly in the lamplight before putting it back.

The blockers left the room and headed to the river ahead of my arrival. Konstantin handed me the semi-auto and holster for my pocket. I took the small revolver and placed it in my special boot holster. I held my shirt up while Carmen deftly strapped the large knife to my torso. I let it drop when she was finished.

"Okay. I'm ready."

She leaned forward and kissed me on the forehead. "Okay. Be careful. We'll be close."

Konstantin gave me a quick hug. "Get moving. Everyone is in position waiting for you." He and Carmen slipped out the door.

I made my way down the stairs, following the faint red glow of the exit sign. I took a deep breath and then pushed the door open.

Chapter 17

The cool night air felt fresh on my skin, but the fear was cold in my chest. I began the six-block trek to the river, my footsteps quiet on the pavement.

Tourists occasionally strolled down the streets near the hotel, but after a few blocks, I saw no one.

I was alone in the dark night. I passed near the beignet café, the river front only a block away. I glanced behind me as I crossed the road.

I saw them.

The reaction in my body was violent. My subconscious grasped the danger before I had a chance to process it. My mind went into instinctive red-alert mode.

Just your average guys at first glance.

But they were anything but. Their steps were jerky and unnatural, as if they didn't know how to operate the body they were walking in. As I paused to watch, they moved ten feet with one step, in a jerky, almost glitchy motion, but with perfect unison. I'd seen it before, the weird movement and felt the strange feelings that came with it. I'd seen it in the trees and shadows of San Antonio.

Cold, unadulterated fear nested at the base of my spine at the realization that accompanied my knowledge. They had been following me for a while.

They wavered and flickered, like reception going bad on a television. I swallowed the scream rising in my throat. They were getting close. Really close.

Oh, shit.

I sprinted. I made it down to the river's edge, avoiding the paved sidewalk where tourists might be.

I glanced behind me again, shocked to see they were only ten feet away from me. I picked up speed, running across the loose rocks in the direction Dennis had instructed.

I pretended to stumble over an old car tire planted by Dennis jutting over the rocks. I fell on my stomach hard, even though it was controlled movement. By the time I flipped over onto my back, they were only a few feet away. I didn't see any of my companions. I pulled out my gun.

A large form jumped out of the long grass lining the bank, beheading one of them in one precise movement of a large machete. I gasped at its head rolled straight to me and came to rest by my side. "Fly, Aurora!" Damien yelled, still holding the machete he had just skillfully used.

I launched myself into the air, away from the other thing. My ascent was violently interrupted. Its hand wrapped around my non-holstered ankle in a crushing grip. The bones in my ankle crunched in a sick way, sending jolts of pain up my leg and into my hip.

Konstantin attacked him from the side, tackling it mid-air. Its hand released my ankle. They both tumbled to the ground. I landed behind the thing, now in earnest battle with Konstantin.

More people spilled out of the brush surrounding us. Dennis pushed me out of the way. Keith caught my arm. He pulled me close to him, and then gently rotated me behind him, creating a barrier between me and the Shyama.

Konstantin had prevailed in his hand-to-hand combat. The creature was pinned to the ground.

Dennis placed a gun with a thick silencer against the skull of the thing and literally blew its head off. The blood and gore splattered on the rocks all around us. Despite what all my training had prepared me for, the sight was shocking.

Within thirty-seconds, both of the Shyama had been incapacitated. I was no longer in immediate danger.

Keith stepped away from me, grabbed a large black duffel bag hidden in the grass, and threw it on the rocks. I looked up, tearing my eyes away from the two decapitated bodies, still shocked from the incredible display of violence and gore. Carmen, Konstantin, Dennis, Karen, Ben, and the other blockers had stepped out of the long grass and formed a loose circle around the bodies. Dennis pulled a large machete out of the black duffel bag. "Quick. Let's finish this."

For every mess, there was a clean up. It was part of the rules. I grabbed a machete out of the bag and joined in with the rest, dispatching the solid forms into much smaller parts.

My brain went into shock as I did the gruesome work. Their bodies looked human, with blood, entrails, and all the other bells and whistles, but something was wrong. They broke into crumbly pieces with little effort. Their flesh was ice cold to the touch, even though they had only been dead for a couple of minutes.

Once their bodies were destroyed, we threw the pieces into the swiftly moving river, except for one. Karen sealed it in a thick plastic evidence bag to take back to the scientists.

I put my hands in the cold water. The swift current rinsed the blood off my hands, dim light painting the red streaks a muted black.

I liked it.

"Karen?" Dennis asked.

She nodded and pulled the backpack off her back. "Okay, who needs a clothing change?"

I looked down and took in the bright smear of blood across my chest and shoulders. Several of the others were covered in blood. I accepted the sweater she threw at me, throwing her my bloody sweater in return, which she crammed into her bag. Several others followed suit, changing into non-bloody clothes. I tried, though not very hard, to avert my eyes from Keith's incredibly well-muscled build as he changed shirts.

When we were all changed, Dennis squinted at all of us in the dark. "Okay. You guys look good. Head back to the hotel. Go in groups of two or three." He ran his fingers through his hair before he spoke again. "Good job."

I walked back to the hotel with Keith, ignoring the throbbing in my ankle and the popping sensation with every step. It had only been fifteen minutes from the time I left the hotel room and stepped out into the cold night air. Remnants of fear still trickled through my body.

Keith wrapped one strong arm around my waist. "I can hear your ankle popping." He pulled me closer. "Are you okay? It was a lot, I know."

"I'm just a little shell shocked." His arm felt good around me. I didn't shrug it off like I should have.

"I'm glad you're with us now. You'll do well."

"Thanks," I said.

He leaned closer. "I watched you clean the blood from your hands in the river. You were excited."

I opened my mouth to protest, but snapped it shut and opted for silence instead.

"It means you're a little wild around the edges. Remember: you are many things, but human is not one of them."

There was acceptance and a little something more in his eyes, but no judgment.

We were the second group to get back to the hotel. Damien and Karen were already there, speaking quietly at the small table in my hotel room. Konstantin and Carmen came shortly, followed by Dennis and Ben. The other three blockers came in the final group.

Keith handed me a small scrap of paper with his name and number written on it. "I don't want this to be the last time we talk." He kissed me on the cheek and walked out of the room with his handler. I folded it and shoved it into my pocket. But I couldn't. Wouldn't. Not yet. Maybe not ever.

Soon, everyone had left the room except for Dennis, Konstantin, and Carmen. Dennis pulled a few beers out of fridge. "I think this calls for a mini-celebration to a successful first mission for Aurora," Dennis said.

We all raised our glasses. The beer was good in my overheated mouth. Carmen and Konstantin sat cross-legged on their bed, all smiles.

A thump brought everyone to attention. A beer bottle was rolling around the ground, bubbling its contents onto the thin carpet. My eyes jumped to Carmen. She was frozen in place, her eyes closed, her hands now empty.

Her bright aqua eyes flew open and she jumped to her feet. "Aurora!"

Konstantin grabbed her arm. "Darling, what is it?"

She ignored him and kept her gaze fixed on me. "It's them. Something's wrong...your mom."

Chapter 18

The world tightened around me. "What?" I said. "What do you mean?"

Before she could answer, Konstantin's cell phone rang. He glanced at the caller ID and flicked it open. "What is it?"

His eyes moved to me as he heard what the caller said. "How many? Where?" he asked the caller, pausing between questions. "We're on our way."

He hung up. "They've been spotted by the people watching your mom." He shut the cell phone and shoved it back in his pocket. "My people are trying to distract them, but they need backup before they go against them. They must have figured out who you are somehow."

My knees gave out and I sank to the floor.

No.

Konstantin kneeled next to me. "You stay here with the blockers. It will be okay I—"

"No!" I said. "I am not staying here with the blockers. We need to leave."

Konstantin put his hand on my arm. "It's not safe."

"Screw that!" I shrugged his arm off. "This is my mom we're talking about here. I don't care if I'm safe. You can sit here and argue about it if you like, but I'm leaving." I grabbed my purse and jacket, ready to head out blindly into the night.

"She's right. We have no time to waste. Let's go," Dennis interjected, giving Konstantin a hard look. "Go to the airport. We'll meet you there. I'll make some calls and get more people to meet us there with weapons." He strode to the door, cell phone in hand. He paused at the doorway. "How many?"

Konstantin hesitated, his eyes darting to me and Carmen. "Five," he finally answered.

Dennis pressed his mouth into a thin line. It scared the living crap out of me to see steel-nerved Dennis worried.

"How much time do we have?" he asked.

"Not much, six, seven hours maybe," Carmen said.

"I'll activate our standby units, but we are the closest."

I glanced behind me as we headed to the stairs. Dennis leaned in the doorway of Keith's room, speaking in low voices to Keith and Damien. Keith's eyes flicked to mine right before I went down the stairs. I hated the pity I saw in them.

I was silent, using my free hand to wipe the tears from my face. I had to get to Wichita. I couldn't let anything bad happen to her.

I barely noticed the engine roaring to life in the rental. All my energy was far away, wishing for a way to transport myself to my mother's side.

Carmen slid in next to me, while Konstantin sped through the empty streets.

Carmen put her arm around me. "I need you to calm down. We'll make it in time. We're going to protect her, okay?" She wiped a tear off my cheek. "You want to call her?"

I counted my breaths in and out, fighting for a calmer place. The panic was there, eating away at the edges, but I was in control again.

I dialed her number. "Mom?" As soon as I heard her voice, I could feel the delicate control already cracking.

"What's wrong?"

"They're after you, and they are close, in Wichita." I choked out the words, losing my fight against the sobs. "This is all my fault. I'm so sorry."

"They found me? Where are you? Are you okay?" Her questions tumbled out.

I was no longer able to speak, my sobs choking my words. A dark swirl of fear and anger wrapped around me, pulling at the very fibers of my sanity.

Carmen took the phone from my hand. "Aubrey? It's Carmen. Yes, she is safe, with us," she said after a pause. "I'm not sure how they found you." She paused, listening to my mom speak.

"It's too late. If you run, it will grab their attention. Plus, it could make it harder for our people to get to you." A much shorter pause. "Use the largest caliber you have. If you can destroy their head, it incapacitates them for several hours."

She handed the phone to me.

"Mom?"

"It's going to be okay."

"It's not okay," I said.

"Do whatever Carmen and Konstantin tell you. I love you."

"I'm so sorry," I whispered.

"It's not your fault, baby. I love you. Stay strong and stay alive, no matter what happens to me."

"Don't say that. I love you."

"I love you more," she answered before she hung up.

We made the next flight to Wichita via Dallas. We boarded immediately.

I leaned my head against the window of the plane, willing it to take off so we could get to Wichita. I glanced at my watch. It was 5:00 a.m. My mind raced a million miles a second, going over every possible scenario. It flashed to my mom, to the Shyama, to Carmen, to Konstantin, to my sister, and to the stupid picture of Gavyn in the magazine.

I woke up when the plane touched down in Dallas. I tapped my feet impatiently while I waited for the plane to make its endless journey to the gate. My ankle was mostly healed and had only the slightest hint of discomfort, a great perk of being one of the gifted.

I jumped out my seat, nearly hitting my head in the process. Carmen put her arm on mine. "She's fine. We can't make the plane go any faster."

Konstantin pulled out his cell phone as soon as we walked off the plane. He snapped the phone shut and spoke to us in a low voice as we make our way to our departing gate. "One of them was in your mom's neighborhood early this morning."

"What?" I stumbled over my tired feet. He caught me before I hit the ground and left his arm around my waist. "Hold on! Please let me finish. Our two blockers took it out. There are only four left now. The rest of the crew in New Orleans are two hours behind us. Some more people are driving over from Texas right now. They are already in south Kansas."

I walked in circles around the perimeter of the gate. People glanced at me then looked away. They were trying not to stare, probably because I was acting crazy. Maybe I was crazy.

"Drink this." Carmen handed me a bottle of water. I gulped the whole thing down. "Now go to the bathroom, wash your face and hands, and get yourself together."

I forced my rubbery legs to walk to the restroom. When I came out of the stall, I confronted my image.

My long hair hung limply around my shoulder and elbows. In the harsh bathroom lights, my skin was pale, and sickly white, with splotches of hot red on my cheeks. I had deep dark circles under my eyes.

I felt an incredible and overpowering surge of anger toward the Shyama. I grabbed onto the anger like a life preserver, pulling it inside of me and using it to focus. They had made me feel this way. They were coming after my mom. They needed to die. I wanted to make them bleed, make them hurt.

I was ready to fight.

Chapter 19

We landed in Wichita two hours later. My brain had shifted into tactical mode. I looked expectantly at Carmen as we landed.

"We need to hurry, but your mom is fine right now."

As we strode off the tarmac, Konstantin was on his cell phone, talking in hushed tones so he wouldn't alarm the crowds of morning travelers streaming by us. He snapped the phone shut and motioned with his finger for me and Carmen to come closer.

"The two blockers are sitting in front of her house in a SUV. The Shyama are in the neighborhood, but they're hiding. The crew from New Orleans will land in about forty-five minutes."

"Can I call her?" I asked.

"If you call your mom when you are this close, it's going to put a beacon on her."

"Okay."

Carmen spoke up. "Let's get food and caffeine. Come on."

"We need to go!"

"Konstantin is getting the rental car, which is going to take a few minutes. I can't make it go any faster. You need fuel."

She hooked her arm through mine and directed me to a fast food restaurant. We loaded up with food and soft drinks the met Konstantin outside, who was waiting in the rental car.

I forced myself to eat while he drove. Dark gray and black clouds gathered in the sky. A serious Midwestern super cell thunderstorm was rolling in.

My anxiety built as we got closer to my mom's house. I couldn't wait to see her face, just to know she was really okay.

Carmen stiffened in her seat, breathing heavily as we pulled onto my mom's street. "They are close. Very close."

We pulled up behind the large black SUV parked in front of the house. Two very tall, Hispanic guys emerged from the SUV as we rolled to a stop. They waited outside my door until I got out, then formed a protective boundary around me while we ran up the long driveway.

My mom yanked open the front door to let all of us in, then slammed it behind us, locking the three extra bolts she had installed on the door years ago.

She pulled me into a hug. "You should have stayed in Orleans. It isn't safe for you," she said, her green eyes probing mine. "Are you okay?"

"I'm okay. Are you?"

A flash of lightening interrupted our reunion. A loud smattering of wind-blown rainwater pattered against the window. Carmen looked out the large window at the ever darkening sky. "This is going to be a nasty one. It's getting dark."

She put her pale hand on the window and closed her eyes. We were all silent as she used her gift. "They are preparing to attack. They're going to use the storm as cover. We need to get ready. Now."

Konstantin turned his attention to my mom. "What do you have?"

She led him over to the couch, where she had laid out her weapons and ammo. Konstantin and my mom had a quick discussion before handing out my mom's impressive collection of handguns. I had always made fun of her for her interest in firearms, but now I understood.

Konstantin and the blockers went methodically through the house, planning a defense and identifying all the entry points.

An impossibly loud boom of thunder shook the house. I peered outside the large ceiling to floor window that dominated the living room. The front lawn was neatly manicured with a row of round shrubs. The storm darkened sky cast everything in deep blue light. Wind gusts shook the branches of the trees with violent force. The familiar scene of my childhood was transformed into a menacing landscape.

As my eyes roamed over the yard, a dark shadow rose above the hedge, barely visible in the swirling rain and darkness.

I could clearly see a head, shoulders, arms, and legs, but it didn't have a face. The inhumanity of it hit me hard. "It's outside."

"Get away from the window!" Carmen screamed.

Before I had time to step back, the window exploded, sending a shower of glass everywhere. Something large, cold, and hard shot through the window, tackling me and pinning me against the far wall of living room. My head made contact with the opposite wall with a loud crack. I struggled to understand how I had traveled fifteen feet in one second. My gun flew out my hand.

It pinned me against the wall, holding me in place with a cold hand around my neck. It squeezed hard, choking off my breath. I stared at the thing in front of me as it drained the life out of me. Where the face should be there was nothing but darkness, a swirling, moving, cluster of black matter. I tried to scream, but I couldn't. I struggled violently, kicking like a mad woman. My head throbbed in pain.

My leg made contact with its body and its grip loosened. The thing made a strange clicking sound, originating somewhere where its face should be. The inhuman noise spurred my fear, and I clawed at its cold unsubstantial strange skin, gouging bloody holes.

One of the blockers pounced on it from behind, sending it to the floor in front of me. Once its grip was released from my throat, I sunk to the ground, gasping for air.

It fought back, throwing the blocker with super-human force out the broken front window.

Konstantin and Carmen jumped on top of it, struggling to keep it down. The third blocker jumped in, pinning it to the ground. It struggled, rapidly flickering like the ones I had seen in New Orleans. "Hurry. I can't keep it from moving for long," Carmen said.

I lunged forward, looking for the gun I had dropped, still gasping for breath. As I clamored on the floor in confusion, five steady shots exploded near my ear. I looked up as my mom lowered her gun. She had delivered the shots precisely to the thing's head, or at least the place where its head used to be. Gore was now splattered over her green couch, ivory wall, and me. Carmen, Konstantin, and the blocker were still pinning its now limp body down, but they were unharmed.

My mom pulled me off the ground. "Are you okay?" she said, her fingers probing the painful spot at the back of my head.

"I think so." My voice was scratchy and weird.

She pressed my dropped gun into my hand. "Try and keep it with you this time, okay?"

"They're coming!" Carmen shouted over the rain and wind now howling through the open window.

Three more hazy, dark figures filled the street, standing in the swirling wind and heavy rain. In perfect unison, they drifted up the length of the long driveway.

A pair of headlights pierced the darkness down the street. The car slammed to an abrupt stop in front of the house and a tall, familiar figure jumped out and started jogging up the driveway.

No!

He was running to the dark figures. He would encounter them in mere seconds, and they would kill him. "Gavyn!"

"Oh no," Konstantin breathed.

I was out the door and zooming to Gavyn before anyone could stop me. I had to at least try to save him.

As I flew forward, the three figures flashed closer to me. I was, for the moment, a complete exposed target that caught their attention.

I was dead meat.

As Gavyn passed within their reach, they froze in their track and began backing away, all in different directions. Their unified movements were gone, their flickering movements muted.

Gavyn reached me. "Aurora," he whispered. He wrapped his arms around me. An ocean of emotion ran through me when his voice reached my ears and his flesh touched mine. He was here, holding me, but we were going to die.

He pushed me behind him, holding his arms out to block me from them. He backed us up, until we were near the house.

One was moving in an erratic, slow, pace down the street. One was standing near the garage, staring dumbly at the wall, the other was still advancing. It flashed and was suddenly within arms reach of me. Gavyn tackled it, pushing it up against the wall.

It threw Gavyn off, sending him alarmingly high into the air and out of my field of vision. Before I could even look to see where he was, it had me pinned to the ground, its strange clicking noises drowning out all the noises around me. Its cold hand pushed into my chest, sinking suddenly unsubstantial fingers into my body.

Freezing cold rushed though me, slowing my heart beat. *So this is how they kill.*

I struggled wildly, trying to gain the slightest inch of wiggle room.

The other Shyama snapped out of their reverie, moving toward me faster than anything should be able to travel.

I brought my knee up, driving my leg into it with all the strength in my body. It was momentarily stunned, releasing its grip enough for me to free my hand. I shoved the gun into the swirling mass of its face and pulled the trigger. Guts exploded all over, filling my mouth with blood. I pushed it off me, coughing as I struggled to stand, searching for Gavyn.

Gavyn was crumpled on the edge of the lawn in a too-still heap, one arm splayed out to the side.

My mom was running toward me, screaming my name. The blockers were following her as the remaining two Shyama closed in.

Konstantin and Carmen poured out of the house. The lawn became a loud haze of rain, thunder, lightening, and flashes of gunfire and glint of knives.

I stumbled to my feet. "Get back in the house!" I screamed at my mom.

"I'll help you get Gavyn!" she yelled over the battle.

The Shyama flashed and re-apparated all over the lawn in a dizzying display of speed. Carmen crumpled to the ground, clutching her shoulder as blood poured from it. She scooted on her butt into the open front door, pain written across her face.

I shared a glance with my mom. We ran to Gavyn across the spinning vortex of shadow and flesh. One of the Shyama tried to tackle us, but I pushed it off, sending it tumbling into Konstantin. He grabbed its arms while one of the blockers hacked its neck with the meanest looking axe I had ever seen, decapitating it in three powerful swings.

"Carmen, she's hurt," I told Konstantin.

"I know. Go to Gavyn. Hurry," Konstantin panted. "We can handle the other one."

I ran to Gavyn, my mom not far behind me.

"Gavyn!" My knees sank into the mud and grass.

"Aurora." His eyes fluttered opened. He grunted and crunched his abs, trying to sit up.

"Slowly," my mom said, gun still raised. She eyed the battle. The blockers had successfully overpowered the remaining Shyama and forced it into the side door of her garage, out of public view. She reluctantly holstered her gun before crouching next to him.

"Does your neck hurt? Can you feel your toes?" she asked him.

"I'm okay. I was unconscious for a minute, I think." He carefully unfolded his body until he was standing. "I'm fine, actually."

He stood in front of us, a tiny smile pulling at the corner of his mouth.

He's okay. He's here.

The world started to spin. Black encroached on the corners of my vision.

"She's passing out," my mother said, but her voice was muted. I couldn't hear much over the roar in my ears.

Gavyn's strong arms wrapped around me. "Careful, don't hurt yourself," my mom said.

I wanted to protest, to tell him to rest and not to carry me, but my lips could not form the words.

Gavyn carried me back into the house through the open front door, past the shocked eyes of my mom who held it open for us. We were both soaked from the heavy rain. He gently lowered me to the floor.

He kneeled next to me, pulling my face closer to his. "I've been looking for you for months. We're supposed to be together. I'm supposed to protect you. I can feel it. Aurora, please. We need to be together." He pulled me closer to him. "Thank God you're okay. I can't live without you. Please, don't leave like that again."

He pulled me into a seated position. "Please say something. Please tell me you're okay."

"Are you really here? Are you really okay?" I whispered.

A huge smile broke out on his face. "Yes. I'm here and I'm fine."

A soft cough brought us out of our reverie. I had forgotten about all the other people in the room, the broken window, the storm, and even the incapacitated Shyama. Gavyn was all I could see. I stood on shaky legs.

Konstantin came in through the door. "Neutralized rather quickly. Gavyn saved us."

"What do you mean?" I asked.

"The handler bond," Carmen said. She was leaned up against the couch while my mom bandaged her arm. "Gavyn."

"Handler?" Gavyn echoed. "What the heck is going on? Does this have something to do your flying thing?"

Konstantin spoke. "We have a lot to explain to you, but yes, your instincts have led you here today for a reason."

Konstantin's cell phone rang, startling everyone. He flicked it open and turned away, muttering into it.

He came back and put his arm around Carmen's shoulders. "Dennis and the crew are down the street. We're going to move this operation into the garage."

"Excuse us." Gavyn grabbed my arm and led me away from the living room, into the first open door he could find. He shut the guest room door behind us, spun me around, and put his hand on my face. His finger traced around my rain soaked forehead, nose, and lips. "Are you okay? I can't believe I'm looking at you right now. I thought I'd lost you forever."

"What are you doing here?"

He rested his palm against my cheek. "What am I doing here? I've been searching for you ever since you ran away. I tried calling you, I tracked down your old friends in San Antonio, but nobody knew where you were. Did you think I didn't want to be with you anymore? That I could walk away from the best thing that ever came into my life?"

"I thought you were afraid. I was trying to protect you," I said. "What about Mira? I saw your picture."

"Oh my," he said with a low chuckle. "You, of all people, should know how the paparazzi are. I went to lunch with her and her fiancé. I gave her a hug as we were leaving and they snapped a shot, cropped her fiancé out, and called us an item." He pulled me even closer. "It's you, Aurora. It's always been you."

I wiped a stupid stray tear off my face. While my arm was raised, he pushed up my sleeve further so he could look at the bracelet. "You never took this off?"

I blushed and nodded as I looked at the now tattered bracelet.

He put the tip of his finger on my chin and brought it up so I met his eyes. "Does that mean you still love me?"

"I love you," I whispered, but my words trailed off and my thoughts were instantly dissolved as his warm lips crushed mine.

We stood there for a long time.

Chapter 20

I took his offered hand, using his arm as an anchor so I could pull myself out of the limo. I sucked in my stomach, awkwardly standing up in my tight dress and ridiculous stilettos.

I wore about ten pounds of makeup, hair extensions, a padded push-up bra and a tight corset carefully arranged around the plunging neckline of my plum colored gown.

I looked hot.

The flashes of light started going off as soon as we emerged. I pasted a smile on my face, though I'm not even sure why I bothered. It was all for him.

Him.

He was mine. I glanced over at his perfect face illuminated in the flash of the cameras.

He still took my breath away. "Thanks for doing this." He spoke through clenched teeth, his smile frozen for the benefit of the cameras recording our every move, anxiously waiting for him to walk down the red carpet.

He leaned close to me, placing his lips against my ear. "You know, if I had it my way, I would have removed that silly, silly dress in the limo. You look amazing, my love."

I giggled, momentarily forgetting the audience. "Thanks." My already shaky knees wobbled as he raised his eyebrows and smiled in a way he only did for me.

A piercing, high-pitched voice ruined our moment. His talented but evil publicist crawled out of the limo right behind us, all business in her simple black cocktail dress and ever present smart phone. She tucked a graying strand of hair behind her ear. "Okay, kids. Stop screwing around. Walk arm in arm down the carpet, but when he talks to the media, take five steps back, out of the shot. Got it?"

"No. I didn't get it the first twenty times you told me."

She threw me a nasty look.

She was very irritated at my presence, well, my existence in general. She had pleaded with Gavyn to keep our relationship a secret from his rabid female fans, but he stubbornly refused. She had asked if he would at least feign an interest in a Hollywood figure, which he also refused. She was stuck with me.

When she found out I was attending the premiere of *Blue Leaf,* she had sent a personal shopper to find me a nice designer dress, shoes, handbag and what she called "foundational" garments to correct the areas of my figure she thought were not up to snuff. She then presented me to an overpriced hair stylist to wrangle my long hair.

After all the primping, I understood why movie stars were so hot. Somewhere underneath the foundation, false eyelashes, hair extensions, body shapers, push-up bras, double sided tape, spray-on tan and a five-thousand dollar vintage designer gown, I looked perfect. Almost too perfect, like an airbrushed, vamped up version of myself.

"You ready?" His musical voice was in my ear again. "Just ignore her. You're with me."

"As ready as I'm ever going to be." Lights danced around my vision from the constant flash of the cameras. I hooked my arm through his as we started down the carpet.

The red carpet ran the length in front of the theatre. One side of the carpet abutted against the outside wall of the theatre, which was plastered with promotional movie posters. The other side was a velvet rope holding back a crushing group of eager cameramen, photographers, and screaming fans.

Reporters leaned over the rope, shouting to grab Gavyn's attention. Voices piled on top of each other with requests for him to look at them for their picture, while various reporters waived microphones, trying to get his attention.

His publicist scanned the sea of photographers with narrowed eyes. She motioned him over to a national entertainment show host who was waving at him. "Go, talk to her. Keep it light."

I unwound my arm from Gavyn's and hung back with his publicist. Troy stood twenty feet away, laughing his big laugh and smiling and waving at all his fans. His easy personality and sunny disposition were perfectly suited for fame.

He spotted me and strode over with a bright smile. Ignoring the press, he pulled me into a big hug. "Hey, Texas! Hot Damn. You look sexy! Gavyn is one lucky man."

"You look pretty darn good yourself." I pulled away to arms length so I could check him out in his tux.

He put his arm around me and faced the cameras, who were constantly flashing during our exchange. "Smile! You're on camera!"

"Gee, thanks."

"Seriously though, I'm glad you're back in his life. Those months you were gone he was miserable. And, well, I may have missed you too."

"I missed you back."

Gavyn appeared at my elbow. "Hey, man, are you trying to steal my date?"

Troy laughed and they embraced with some manly back pounding. The photographers went crazy. The evil publicist hissed at me. "Five steps." I tried not to roll my eyes as I stepped out of the shot.

Gavyn returned to fetch me later, keeping firmly by my side for the rest of his interviews. Per the publicist's instructions whispered into my ear, I did not say a word.

Twenty-five excruciating minutes later, we were seated and watching the movie. I spent most of the movie watching the lights dance across Gavyn's perfect face. I was thrilled to notice he spent most of the movie watching me too.

Life had been good since I moved to Los Angeles.

I had settled into Gavyn's awesome townhome in the hills over the past few weeks. It was modest and tucked away safely behind gates, so he didn't have paparazzi bothering him. I loved the huge canopy bed, the large deck and the gleaming marble counters. I often found myself wandering around the cool wood floors staring at the vaulted ceilings, the chandelier, the built in Jacuzzi, and the surrounding Hollywood hills out the window. I still couldn't believe I lived there.

Living with Gavyn was easy. Really easy. First of all, he still knocked my socks off every time I saw him. After the several months of not seeing each other after my exposure, we appreciated our alone time together. A lot.

Gavyn nudged me, startling me out of my reverie. "You ready?"

"Um, that's it? We walk down a red carpet, look pretty, then we're done?" I took his offered arm as we filed out of the theatre.

He chuckled. "Not so fast. We have to go the release after-party. There will be another red carpet there, plus press inside. You're stuck with me for a few more hours."

"Oy." My feet were killing me and I could feel the weight of the makeup on my face. The only thing I wanted to do was take a long shower, wash off my makeup, and change. "Please tell me there is at least going to be alcohol, preferably free, and preferably strong."

His publicist's shrill voice answered me. Where did she even come from? "Yes. But you may not have more than two drinks. Try not to act like a total lush."

I spent the next three hours following Gavyn around the release party. Despite his publicist's warnings, I took four tequila shots. I would have preferred beer, but I was afraid to drink that much volume for fear I would explode out of my dress, and not in the sexy wardrobe malfunction way.

By the time it was 11:00, I was teetering around in my silly stilettos, flushed deep red, and giggling too much.

Gavyn guided me to the back door. "Okay, love, let's go. You look a little too cheery."

I said nothing, but thought my hiccup in response sufficed as a yes.

I sobered up by the time we returned home. I went into the bathroom and removed the bobby pins. My brown hair tumbled around my elbows, grazing the middle of my back. I took a long hot shower, scrubbing until I could no longer feel the cake of makeup on my face.

When I got out, I changed into shorts and a tank top. I glanced at my reflection in the mirror. It wasn't as pretty as the red-carpet version of me, but it was me.

"Welcome back." Gavyn came up behind me and wrapped his arms around my waist.

"Sorry your glamazon is gone."

"Oh no, I much prefer this." He kissed me on the check. "Come on the back patio. I made you some lemonade. It's nice outside."

I followed him outside, settling into one of two rocking chairs. The chair creaked as he sat down next to me.

We rocked in the cool breeze, the rockers ticking off the seconds in uneven time.

Gavyn took my hand, and held it to his lips. "For you," he said, before opening my hand and pushing something cold and hard into it.

I opened my hand and stared at it. It was a shiny gold ring, with intricate knots carved around the outside.

"Look at the engraving," Gavyn prodded.

I tilted the ring back in forth in my hand until the moon hit the right angle and I saw the words flash. "Vita mea, amor meus," I said out loud.

"My life, my love," he translated.

"Oh, Gavyn, it's so pretty and shiny and sweet. Thank you. I don't…what's this for?"

I looked up. Gavyn was kneeling in front of my chair.

"It's your wedding ring. Marry me?"

My eyes flicked down to the ring and back up to his face. He was staring at me anxiously, his shoulders tense around his ears.

I slipped the ring on my left finger and cleared my throat. "Done."

He pulled me out of the chair. I snuggled against his chest and held him as we swayed together in our mutual joy. Nothing could ever ruin my perfect fairy tale moment.

And then my phone rang. Not my regular cell, but the one that I only used for the organization.

"Damn," I said.

"Better get it."

I answered it.

"Sorry to bother you."

"Konstantin." My voice was flat.

"I am sorry. We have an emergency. We're outside your house. Both of you need to come now."

I hung up the phone and turned to Gavyn. "We're on, something big."

"Okay."

I pulled on jeans, grabbed my purse and gun, and waited by the door for him.

He took my hand as he met me at the door, pressing the cool metal of my new ring to his cheek. "I love you."

"I love you too."

We stepped into the swirling darkness. He wrapped his fingers around mine as we walked together into our now entwined future, whatever it may be.

Acknowledgements

FLEE is how it all started for me. Back in 2008, I was exhausted after a long day at work, drinking wine in my cramped apartment, crumbling under the pressure from work and my ballooning student loan debt and bills. I picked up my laptop and typed "Chapter 1." In the six weeks that followed, I frantically wrote a story about Aurora and Gavyn, in what would many years and several re-writes (and title changes) later, become FLEE. After I finished FLEE, I never stopped writing, and probably never will.

Many good friends and family encouraged me in those early days: April, Juvie, Brooke, Laura, Raymond, Rex, Danielle and Dennis. I thank you all from the bottom of my heart. Without your encouragement and critical feedback, I never would have continued on this journey.

To my beta readers Audrey Burns, Melinda Scott-Mendoza and Veronica Webster, you guys rock. I'm so thankful.

Many thanks Regina Wamba of Mae I Design for the amazing cover.

I'm so thankful to you, reader, for choosing this book. Thank you from the bottom of my heart.

Other works by Miranda Kavi

CRUX, The Aurora Lockette Series Book 2

The RUA series
RUA (Book 1)
RIVE (Book 2)

A girl with an unknown destiny.

A boy from a hidden world.

When Celeste starts at a new school in a small, Kansas town, she hears whispering voices, has vivid nightmares, and swarms of blackbirds follow her every move. She is oddly drawn to aloof Rylan, the other new student who has his own secrets.

The exact moment she turns seventeen, she wakes to a bedroom full of strange creatures, purple light emanating from her hands, and Rylan breaking in through her bedroom window.

He knows what she is . . .

Intriguing and deeply romantic, *RUA* is page-turning YA novel with a supernatural twist.

About the Author

Miranda Kavi is a romance and paranormal fiction author. Her books have been listed on the top 100 best seller lists on Amazon and iTunes. She has worked as an attorney, an executive recruiter, and an assistant in a biological anthropology lab. She loves scary movies, museums, and is hopelessly addicted to chocolate. She lives in Houston with her husband and daughter

Want to learn more? Find me here!

http://mirandakavi.net/

http://www.facebook.com/MirandaKavi

http://twitter.com/mirandakavi

CPSIA information can be obtained at www.ICGtesting.com
Printed in the USA
LVOW13s1449130414

381505LV00006B/761/P

9 781480 266827